Catch
A Falling
Clown

Catch A Falling Clown

A TOBY PETERS MYSTERY
BY STUART M. KAMINSKY

St. Martin's Press
New York

Copyright © 1981 by Stuart M. Kaminsky
For information, write: St. Martin's Press,
175 Fifth Avenue, New York, N.Y. 10010
Manufactured in the United States of America

Library of Congress Cataloging in Publication Data

Kaminsky, Stuart M.
Catch a falling clown.

I. Title.
PS3561.A43C3   813'.54   81-14607
ISBN 0-312-12377-9   AACR2

10 9 8 7 6 5 4 3 2 1
First Edition

1/28/82

This one is for
Gar Simmons and his clan

Catch
A Falling
Clown

The gorilla was sleeping.

When he woke up he'd find a clown in his cage. There would be no reasoning with Gargantua. He was not a reasonable gorilla. Maybe there *are* no reasonable gorillas. This was the only nonhuman one I had ever met, and if fate didn't step very gently in and let me out, it was the only gorilla I would ever meet.

His keeper had told me that Gargantua was so mean that they had to throw live snakes into his cage just to get him to move out so they could clean the floors.

"But gorillas, they don't eat people," said the keeper, a knotty twig named Henry Yew. "That is a misnomer. They rends 'em apart or chomps 'em sometimes, but they don't eat 'em."

So when Gargantua woke up looking for some succulent head of cabbage to bend or chomp, he would find instead a private detective named Toby Peters. With the war in the Pacific going badly and reports of the Japanese bombing Los Angeles and Seattle, I'd just make a curiosity item in the entertainment section of the *Los Angeles Times:* FAMOUS CIRCUS

GORILLA RIPS PRIVATE DETECTIVE. Maybe the *Times* would wonder why I had been in his cage dressed as a clown. Maybe not.

Well, what the hell, forty-six isn't a bad age to go out at. Not quite getting old, but sure as hell not young. If I survived the night in the cage, my back would probably be sore, and the killer I had been tracking would be gone.

Maybe that great black ball of fur would stay asleep through the night. He looked like a peaceful drunk with his arms out, palms up, his back against the wall of the cage, and his mouth slightly open. He smelled like a musty closet, but I probably smelled worse.

I didn't have much hope of outsmarting him when those eyes opened. Given what had happened over the last three days, he was almost certainly smarter than I was.

The cage was in the corner of a side tent. A lion in the cage nearby lay with his head on his paws, watching me and purring. A breeze from outside sent ripples across the canvas and made a "guwhump-guwhump" sound. Through the open flap of the tent I could see the dark outline of a wagon and the open field in which the circus had been put up. In the moonlight, I could also see the frozen furrows of the truck tracks. In the morning, when the sun came out and the circus began to shrug awake, the thin layer of ice would be crushed or melt away, and the field would again be a sea of mud. The big cat watching me grew restless and yawned or howled sadly. Gargantua stirred, swatted an imaginary fly in his sleep, groaned a few echoes below sea level, and was quiet.

I could have yelled. Maybe someone would have heard me. Even if they did, I sure as hell would wake my cellmate.

I'd been told Gargantua didn't like clowns. Actually, Gargantua didn't seem to like much of anything or anybody. He had his own air-conditioned and heated cage and people left him somewhat alone, but he pined for the veldt or wherever the hell gorillas come from. I made a decision. I'd take off my clown makeup.

I rubbed at the makeup with my sleeve and considered

taking the offensive. There was a tire in the cage that Gargantua snapped like a rubber band when he got bored. It was a better tire than the retread quartet I had on my elephant-battered 1934 Buick. What if I lifted the tire, slipped it over his furry head and shoulders, and then started to scream for help? Maybe it would hold him long enough. Like hell it would. A few more minutes or hours of smelling the air, feeling the chill of night, and wondering how all this happened had more appeal than trying to straitjacket the snoring hulk across from me.

Wouldn't it be grand if he woke up and had a rusty nail stuck on his behind? I'd scramble over, coo something to him, pull off the offending fragment, and we'd be buddies forever. Yes, and the Nazis would apologize and pull out of Belgium.

Less than a week earlier, I had packed my single suitcase with my extra crumpled suit, two pair of socks, my last white shirt, and a couple of pairs of underwear whose holes might be worth a few laughs to a Peeping Tom. It wasn't that I didn't have enough money to put my closet in order. I'd just come off a case that brought my bankroll up to almost two hundred dollars after rent and sundry bills. Now, that may not have been much of a cushion for most working Americans in February of 1942, but for me two hundred bucks was the top of the world. What I didn't have was time. The telegram had said hurry, and hurry I had. I begged an extra few gallons of gas from my unfriendly neighborhood mechanic, no-neck Arnie, who figured gas was going to get tight and prices would go through the roof.

"Wouldn't be surprised if someday we pay fifty, sixty cents a gallon of gas," he had said, pointing his cigar at me.

The Buick had taken more paint than Nita Naldi trying to make a comeback. There was so much lead on it that it should have been bullet proof, which I knew from experience was not the case. The present paint job was most patriotic. It was supposed to be a sleek shiny green but looked more like a rotten olive drab. I had no unsolicited offers to buy it, but it moved and complained only when it had reason.

I had stopped only once on the way down the coast from

Los Angeles. That was to negotiate for a full tank of gas by telling the kid operating the pump, who looked six years old, that I was a special representative of Eleanor Roosevelt, that I was touring the area to determine which small businesses needed immediate federal support. The kid paid no attention. It wasn't his station, and he was going in the army in a few days. I was doing my act for the exercise, but in my business you have to keep in practice. You can't tell good lies unless you practice lying a lot. Sometimes I lie when there's no reason for it, just to see if I can get away with it. I had always thought it was a peculiarity of my profession until I ran into an actor who told me actors do the same thing. Then a cop told me that cops lie, and a grocery clerk told me . . . I thought of asking the kid at the pump how good a liar he was, but his eyes were off in the direction of the Pacific Ocean and he was listening to the sound of battleships two thousand miles away.

When I got back on the road I listened to Fibber McGee and Molly as the night folded in. McGee was hiding a horse in the garage. He didn't want Molly to know he had it. His idea was that a horse would be cheaper and more patriotic than a car. I'd been on a horse once. Didn't like it. Molly wound up falling in love with the horse, and I wondered if the horse would be part of the show for a while. The announcer told me that I'd be helping America defeat the Japs and Nazis if I kept my car polished with Johnson's Wax. It would make my car last longer and keep me from having to buy a new one.

I caught up with the circus outside of Mirador, a little town not far from Laguna Beach, off the Pacific Coast highway. Through Santa Monica, Torrance, and Long Beach, I had a prickly feeling of where I was headed. By Newport Beach, I was sure of it. The sheriff of Mirador was named Mark Nelson. Nelson was a wiry little guy who smelled like a weak onion, wore sweaty lightweight suits and fake grins, and didn't like me even a little bit. Less than a year before, I'd made him look bad on a case that had brought me to Mirador. He wasn't happy about this happening in front of the state police and the local talent, mostly the Mexicans who arrived in Mirador pretending they were American migrant workers and had to pay him off. It was the rich folks who lived on the private estates down by the beach who needed the image of a sheriff who made no mistakes. It was the rich folks who paid a little extra to get special attention from Sheriff Nelson and his deputy Alex, a bull of a man Nelson had recruited from among the Mexican workers. Alex went about the job of removing headlights and heads according to Nelson's needs and wishes. Alex did it without betraying feeling or interest. It was a job, like picking lettuce, and he wasn't going to risk it by letting anyone know how he might feel.

I had been a piece of lettuce for Alex once, and I didn't look forward to another meeting with him or the charming sheriff of Mirador, but a job is a job.

The highway sign had said that the circus was in Aldriech Field, but I wasn't going to find Aldreich Field in the dark without some directions. I hit Mirador about ten. The town had tucked itself in and gone to bed with its collective head under the blanket, hoping that when the Japanese decided to land their hordes on the coast, it would be somewhere north or south of Mirador. They had some reason to hope that the sight of the coastline of Mirador would deter an invasion. Once it promised to be the fun center of California. Some big dirty money back in the late 1920s had been washed through clean names, and construction had begun on a series of oceanfront gambling houses, hotels, restaurants, and palaces of dubious amusement. The framework and fronts had been finished when 1929 hit, and the market screamed and died. The workers left Mirador with the money and tools, and the gulls perched at night on the frames of never-to-be-built palaces. Then the wind spit seawater at the partially finished buildings for over a decade, and people forgot what had been a promise. An invasion of Mirador would have confused the Japanese. They would have wondered how the Nazis beat them to it and bombed the place.

From the rubble, Sheriff Nelson and a few others had salvaged enough to make a living by offering Mirador as a place where no questions would be asked if a price was paid.

That was where the circus had stopped and where I now found myself. I drove into the big circle in the center of town, avoided something that may have been alive in the street, and parked alongside a police car in front of Hijo's, the only place in town with its lights on. I could hear the music of a Mexican band playing "La Paloma" from inside when I stepped out of my car. There were no streetlights in Mirador. It wasn't just wartime caution. There had never been any streetlights in Mirador.

I examined myself in the window of the darkened Mirador police station, a storefront next to Hijo's. There wasn't much light, but I could see all I wanted to see, a not very tall, dark man with a flat nose and a rumpled suit. I pulled at the suit to shake or shame it into some embarrassed dignity, but there was no more chance of that than of my face being taken for that of a priest on a pilgrimage.

I followed the music through the doors of Hijo's. There were three people at the bar, a woman with a few extra pounds and two men next to her. The music was coming from a radio, not from a band, and the bartender was sitting behind the bar with his head in both hands and a cigarette drooping from his chubby lips. He looked as if he were thinking about doves in a place he hadn't seen. At one of the three wooden tables, a guy lay dead or drunk with his cheek in a pool of wet amber that I hoped was beer. There wasn't much light, just a few dim bulbs in the ceiling and a neon Falstaff beer sign sputtering on the wall. The fat woman looked over at me. The bartender didn't budge, and the two lotharios didn't seem to notice me.

"A beer," I said, stepping to the bar, tilting back my hat and plunking down a quarter.

The bartender looked at me through the smoke without moving his head. Then he grunted and rose. He was in no hurry.

"I'm with the circus," I said. "Been out setting things up down the line. Can you tell me where to find them?"

"The circus," said the bartender dreamily.

"The circus," I repeated, taking the beer, which he handed

me in the bottle. The bottle wasn't quite warm, but it was a hemisphere away from cool.

"In the field," he said, nodding his head toward the door.

I nodded knowingly, as if he had told me something valuable, and gulped down some beer. I thought I tasted something solid coming out of the bottle but ignored it and tried again.

"Right," I said. "And how do I get to this field?"

The bartender shrugged.

"The other side of town," came the voice of one of the two men with the woman. He stepped away from her and looked at me floor to hat, deciding what should be done with me.

"OK," I grinned. "And how do I get to the other side of town?"

"You turn your ass around, go through that door, and start knocking on doors till someone tells you or shoots you," the man said, stepping toward me. He was bulky, dark, and drunk. His shirt was faded flannel and his pants denim with white patches at the knees.

I looked at the bartender to try to figure out why I had been given such a warm greeting, but he had gone back to his position with head on hands. "La Paloma" played on.

"Hey," I said, taking in another third of the beer, "I'm just a working man looking for his job. I'm not after trouble."

The guy in the faded shirt was a few feet in front of me now, and his mouth was open, revealing about six teeth and a pit of darkness. I knew a dentist who would like to get his grubby fingers on that mouth, but I wanted no part of it.

"That circus ain't for our kids," he said. "The farm kids and rich kids down the beach. They going to your circus."

"Come on, Lope," cried the woman down the bar in a voice that couldn't decide if it was a tenor or a soprano. It continued to crack as she said, "The circus don't cost that much. Your kids could go."

"Fifty cents," I said with a smile.

"And what about the popcorn and stuff they want?" he challenged, breathing something stronger than beer in my face.

The Falstaff sign crackled and we all looked at it, but it

didn't go out. The amber dead man at the table stirred and rolled over to soak the other cheek. I didn't turn my other cheek. I finished my beer, put it on the counter and spoke.

"Say it costs a buck for the whole thing," I said. "I figure that's the cost of two tequilas and a beer. How much you sunk into your own entertainment tonight, pal?"

It was the wrong thing to say. Maybe it came a little bit from getting into the role of circus front man. Maybe it was from being tired from a long trip. Maybe I was just nervous about being back in Mirador. Fighting with a drunken leather-muscled field worker wasn't going to get me directions to the circus.

His face was a thought ahead of his actions. His right arm cocked back, and I reached for the empty bottle. Before the thick fist came around, I whacked the bottle against the side of his head just above the right eye. There was no shattering of glass, just a thunk, and the bulk in front of me went down against the bar.

The other man at the bar rushed toward me and stopped a few feet short when I showed the bottle in my hand. He was smaller than the first guy, about my size and weight, and dressed in black pants with matching shirt and sweater. The bartender roused himself from his dream and looked at me with distaste. He wanted no trouble. He wanted nothing. "La Paloma" ended, and a voice came out of the radio in rapid-fire Spanish.

The flannel bulk was out against the bar, probably as much from what he had soaked away as from my tap on his head. A dark lump was closing his right eye.

"No more trouble," I said to the advancing man, whose eyes were shifting around for something to hit me with or throw at me.

"You hit Lope," he said evenly through his teeth.

"He was going to hit me," I explained, holding tightly to my beer bottle. "Hey, I came in here to find the circus, not to take on a tag team."

Lope's friend grabbed a bottle from the table where the

drunk lay dreaming. His bottle was bigger than mine and had something left in it. The something dripped out as he stepped carefully toward me, eyeing Lope in the hope that the bigger man would get up and join him.

"If this happens at every town along the line, I swear I'm quitting the circus," I said, backing toward the door.

The fat woman at the end of the bar let out a howl of laughter and pounded the bar, sending a whiskey glass tumbling to the floor.

"Let the man alone, Carlos," she said, her voice jumping all over the place. "He's a funny man."

"Lope?" Carlos said, pointing his bottle at his downed drinking companion and drenching himself in alcohol.

"Lope asked for what he got," she said, getting off her stool and looking at me. Carlos looked at the sleeping drunk and the bartender for support, but there was none. He wasn't going to face me without an appreciative audience. He drained the last few drops of the bottle and backed against the bar.

"Mister," said the woman, "I'm what passes for the town whore, and if I wasn't drunk I wouldn't say it."

"Right," I said a few feet from the door. "Thanks."

"Lope ain't a bad guy," she said. "He works hard, got a big family, five kids. He deserves a drunk. Got no education."

"I should have kept my mouth shut," I admitted.

"You *tiene razón* man," she laughed. "You got time for a drink?"

"No, thanks," I said. "I'm expected at the circus."

"Back to the highway," she said with a nod of her head. "Turn right. Look for Carroll Road. Turn right again and go about a mile. You'll see it."

She stepped forward where it was lighter, and she looked less fat than plump. Her teeth were white and even, and her face was smooth and smiling.

"Maybe there's time for one drink more," I smiled.

Lope groaned on the floor and tried to sit up.

"I don't think so now," said the woman. "Lope ain't gonna be happy when he gets up. His brother is deputy sheriff."

"Alex?" I said.

"You know Alex?" she shot back. Even the barkeeper perked up. Alex was a name to reckon with in Hijo's.

"We met once," I said. "Maybe I'll come back for that drink, Miss . . ."

"Alvero, Jean Alvero," she said. "And maybe you better not come back. I think it might even be better if you just go on up ahead and not get together with your circus in Mirador."

"Maybe you're right," I answered and backed out of the door as Carlos bent to help a groggy, one-eyed Lope to his feet.

There is something about me that brings out the worst in dogs, cats, and humans. Something in me is a challenge. I used to think I was cursed. A woman who said she was a witch once put a curse on me. The woman was my own aunt, but her daughter, my cousin, who claimed she was a more powerful witch, supposedly took the curse off, which gives you some indication of my family tree. Curses aside, I think it is simply my face coupled with an uncontrollable urge to bring people to life by prodding them a little. My father wanted me to be a doctor. I've got the curiosity, but not the ambition.

I got into my car and backed out with the lights out. I scraped the police car parked next to me with a sickening scraaatch, turned on my lights, and headed back toward the highway.

Had I but known that three days later I'd be in a cage with a gorilla, I probably would have remained and taken my chances with Lope and Alex; but half the fun of being alive is not knowing what tomorrow will bring. The other half comes by pretending that you don't care.

I found the circus in Aldreich Field without much trouble. It was a huge, dark series of tents, the largest one a central big top with a flag, a bunch of trucks, and mobile wagons. The dark outline of a train with a few dozen cars formed a rear wall behind the scene.

I followed the road to the closest tent, turned off into the mud, and got out to find the man who had hired me. The circus looked like a bunch of black paper cutouts, the kind of thing you'd pick up at the drugstore for a six-year-old whose parents you were visiting. There was even a radio sound-effects record to go with the picture, something right out of "I Love A Mystery." Howling wind across the field, the murmur of animals, voices laughing, and someone raising someone else two bits on a poker hand behind one of the cutouts.

I made my way around mud holes, wagon ruts, footsteps, and debris to the nearest wagon with a light on. I knocked. Voices inside were arguing. I knocked again.

"A minute," came a male voice with a European accent I couldn't place.

The door swung open. It was a few feet above me, and at first all I could see was another black cutout against sudden light. This one looked vaguely like a man.

"Yes?" he said, looking down at me. My eyes adjusted and began to make out the man and another figure behind him. The man in the door was wearing a red velvet robe. His hands were in his pockets. His head was a mane of bright yellow hair over a smooth face; his voice suggested more years than the front showed. Behind him at a table sat a young man looking toward me, a thin, pale, yellow-haired imitation of the man at the door.

"Yes?" he repeated.

"I'm trying to find somebody," I said.

"I am somebody," he replied, pointing to his chest. "I am Sandoval."

I was clearly supposed to know who Sandoval was, but my face must have made it clear that I didn't.

"Sandoval of the great cats," he explained. "My picture is on the posters. My animals are the most wild. Frank Buck and Clyde Beatty are not even amateurs compared to Sandoval."

"Oh, that Sandoval," I said, trying to get the conversation moving before I sank any deeper into the mud. "I'm looking for someone with the circus, someone I'm supposed to meet."

I told him who I was looking for, and he gave me directions on how to get there. The kid at the table behind him listened, his eyes not on me but on the back of Sandoval, whose directions to me were a little vague.

. . . II

"Good enough?" asked Sandoval, throwing his mane back.

"Thanks," I said. "Good night."

"Good night," said Sandoval and then, over his shoulder, "Shockly, bid the man good night."

The boy at the table half rose and said a weak good night. Sandoval sighed enormously and threw out his hands before whispering to me in a voice that could not only be heard by the boy but by anyone within a football field's length.

"The war has made a ruin of all human endeavor," he said. "We can get only apprentice boys with names like Shockly who must be taught even the minimal touches of confidence and pride."

Sandoval had enough confidence and pride for the kid, the U.S. Marines, and the entire USC football team, but I nodded in professional agreement as he closed the door.

I made half a dozen wrong turns in the dark and stepped into something I didn't want to think about before I found myself back at my car. I was tempted to curl up in the back seat, but the last time I had done that my back had been so sore in the morning that I couldn't straighten up.

So I returned to my search. This time I ran into two frail figures side by side. I took them for late-night lovers at first, but when I stepped in front of them I realized that their union was even more permanent than love. They were Siamese twins joined at the hip and wearing a single giant coat to keep out the night.

They were used to seeing faces a lot more frightening than mine around a circus, and they gave me good directions on how to find my client. They also told me their names were Cora and Thelma. I thanked them and went on my way, wondering how the two of them had managed to carry on the whole conversation with both of them saying every word as if I were talking to an echo.

Three minutes later I was at the right railroad car, knocking. Someone inside said, "Hold it," and a few seconds later the door opened and a voice with a Missouri twang said, "Yes?"

"Peters," I said. "Toby Peters."

A hand came down and took mine. "Kelly," he said. "Emmett Kelly."

He helped me up out of the night and into the warm light of his room.

chapter 2

Someone had electrocuted an elephant. There was no doubt about that. The wrinkled gray bulk lay on its side, feet out, trunk curled down, eyes closed. A single night-light cast shadows on his feet, and the maybe of a breeze made the sparse wiry hairs of his body bend and shiver. I have seen humans lying dead. Even when the death was bloody or crazy, it always seemed part of something natural that made me angry, not sad. And here was this smelly mass of an animal filling me with sorrow.

"Something really sad about it," said Kelly at my side. I looked at him and could see that he was talking about himself as well as me.

Kelly was about my size, receding hairline, a nose like Bob Hope's, and a mouth that moved easily into a warm grin. His shoulders were slightly stooped and his chest thin. He was about my age, maybe a year or two younger, and there was a look on his face that made it clear that he was carrying something he wanted help with.

After I had entered his train car, Kelly had excused himself from Tiny Tyne, a plump fellow clown he had been playing rummy with, introducing me not as a private detective but as a friend of a friend looking for a job.

"What was that all about?" I asked as he led the way across the field.

"Sorry, Mr. Peters," he whispered. "I don't know if what I think is happening is happening, and I'm not putting my neck out till I know." As we walked, stepping around shadows and footprints of mud, he told me about the circus.

The Rose and Elder Circus was a thin idea held together by favors, hope, and a few dollars from the hardware empire of Joshua R. Rosenbaum, the Rose and the angel. His investment was on the verge of nightmare, which is somewhere between Palm Springs and Mirador. It was an after-the-season show put together from acts, crew, and equipment rented from the big shows that had ended their seasons. Rose and Elder's biggest attractions were Kelly the clown and Gargantua the gorilla from Ringling. Kelly had gone along for the one-month run as a favor to Elder, an old friend.

The show was a patchwork of acts on the way up and on the way down, grifters and grafters, refugees and runaways. The doctor for the show was over eighty, some of the acts couldn't speak English, and about half of the crew had never seen a circus before.

In spite of this, Elder, whose idea the whole thing was, had managed to put on a circus, three rings, popcorn, peanuts, elephants, and sideshows. He had a dozen trailers, seven trucks, and fifteen railroad cars.

"In here," Kelly said, pointing the way with his lantern, and in I went.

The elephant lay in a corner, and we simply looked at him in silence for a few minutes.

"What makes you think someone killed him?" I said.

"Her; this bull's a female," he said.

"Bull?"

"All elephants are called bulls in the circus," he explained. "She was a good one. Two years ago, ten Ringling elephants died of arsenic poisoning in Atlanta. Police said it was an accident. Last year, there was a fire in the elephant tent when we were in Kansas. Lost another dozen."

"But . . ." I tried.

"Look," he said and walked behind the dead animal where he lifted a piece of canvas. I followed him and found myself looking into a gray dead eye of the elephant. It was hard to force my eyes away to the sight under the canvas.

"What's that?" I said.

"Wires, rigging for tent lights. All attached to that pole where this bull was tied with a metal chain. Someone just touched the two wires together, and she went down. I was in here when it happened, and I saw a little spark. So I went over when they called the doc. Someone had gotten to the pole and pulled the wire off. Must have seen me coming and backed off before they could hide it. I couldn't prove anything, so I just shut up when the doc said the elephant had a heart attack."

I looked down at the mass of wire, which meant nothing to me, and then at the man who held the lantern.

"It's more than the elephants," I said.

"More than the elephants," he said. "Whoever did this saw me coming to check the wires. I think they know I'm thinking more than they want me to think. Truck went wild yesterday, almost ran me down. Driver was off having a sandwich when it happened. It might have been an accident."

"OK, but why would anyone want to kill the elephants?" I asked, keeping my eyes from those of the bull behind me.

"We've got maybe forty elephants in this circus," he said, the lantern light sending shadows to his face that suggested the face of a clown or a skull. "An elephant normally costs fifty thousand dollars. Something like that. Kill off the elephants and you haven't got much of a circus. Damn, you can't even replace elephants with the war on."

We both looked at the dead elephant for a few more seconds and headed toward the entrance to the tent.

"What do they do with a dead elephant?" I said.

"Don't know," sighed Kelly, stepping into the night.

"Don't want to know. What I want to know is who is trying to ruin this circus and maybe kill me."

"In reverse order," I said.

"Together," he corrected. "It's too late to meet people. You can start in the morning. What can you do?"

He stopped and looked at me.

"I can start asking questions and try to find someone with a motive for trying to . . ."

"No, I mean what can you do that would fit in a circus?"

I thought about it for a minute. I could fire a pistol, but not very well. I could take a punch but had already taken too many of them. I . . . "Nothing I can think of," I said.

"I'll think of something in the morning," Kelly said. "Don't talk in front of Tiny. Tiny's a good enough guy, not a bad clown, but he's a talker. I'll get you some cherry pie when we get up."

"Cherry pie?" I said, following him up the stairs of the train car.

"Circus for easy work," he said.

"Right," I said, following him up the three metal steps.

Our footsteps clanged across the field and echoed back at us from the nearby railroad cars. Kelly stopped at the top and looked back.

"I like it at night like this," he said. "You look out and know what's under those tents and in those wagons, and you can't believe that tomorrow it's all gonna be moving and that you're going to be out in front of thousands of people, well, maybe hundreds. It's like another world you know is there and can't believe will come out." He shrugged and stepped into the railroad car.

Tiny was still there. There was an extra mattress in the wagon. Kelly wanted to sleep on it, but I told him a hard mattress on the floor was good for my bad back.

The two clowns played rummy under a small, yellow-bulbed lamp, and I took off my jacket and shirt, scratched my stomach and felt my stubbly face. Kelly told me where to find soap, water, and a towel. It had been a light day. I had done some driving, laid out a drunk in a tavern, met a clown or two, and examined a murdered elephant. I expected the days to get busier and was bothered by the fact that I felt tired. Somewhere in my battered suitcase back in my battered car was a toothbrush whose bristles sagged like a forgotten Christmas tree and a can of Dr. Lyon's tooth powder that would have done me no harm, but I wasn't up to it. I lay back on the mattress with my arms under the thin pillow and looked at the wooden ceiling. Tiny asked me a question, which I answered with a lie before I fell asleep.

Dreams, I've discovered, come in threes. I can usually remember the first two, and I always feel that it is the third one, the one I can't remember, that will really tell me something. In my first dream, I was wandering through the streets of Cincinnati. Everything was red, bright red, not the red of blood but the red of good-smelling new bricks. Even the cars were red. As usual in my dreams, there were no people in Cincinnati but me. I walked into a row house and closed the door behind me, suddenly scared, not of what was inside, but of something outside. Then someone or something knocked at the door. I didn't want to open it. I knew what was on the other side. A clown would be on the other side. Not my old friend Koko, but a six-foot clown with a grinning face. Who needs a clown at your door? Nothing's funny about a clown.

"Who's there?" I said, holding one foot against the door.

"I have a message," came the high voice from the other side of the door.

"Yeah," I said, trying to make it sound tough.

"Life is a circus," came the high voice.

"A circus?"

"Yes," he said. "Usually that means living is fun. But a circus is hard work, blisters to make a few minutes look funny, dangerous, or interesting."

"Then life is a circus?" I asked, looking around for someplace to hide.

He didn't answer. I knew he was looking for another way in.

In my nightmare I told myself I was having a nightmare, but that didn't make it better. I told myself to wake up, but I couldn't. I think I whimpered, and then I was in another dream, a dream I'd rather not talk about. Then the third dream I can't remember. But when I was safely in dream number three, I found myself back in Cincinnati, back in the house with the door. "Wait," I said or thought, "this isn't fair."

"Open the door," came the high clown voice. "Open up."

"No," I cried, trying to wake up, making the effort. I opened my eyes and found myself facing the grinning face. The voice came out of it, the clown voice.

"That's right," he said, leaning over me. "Open them up."

Sheriff Mark Nelson of Mirador was kneeling next to my mattress, dressed in a white suit tapped with spots of sweat. Maybe he thought it was natty to wear sweat-spotted suits. His hat was in his hand, and his thumb was rubbing the dark sweatband. I looked around for Alex the deputy, and my mind was read.

"I told Alex to wait outside," said Nelson. "I wanted to renew our acquaintanceship. Nice, crisp, brisk day outside," he sighed. "Good air round here."

"You want me to move to Mirador," I said, trying to sit up.

"Have to spruce you up a bit if it came to that," he said. "You smell like a Mex field hand."

I was awake now and making no attempt to resist scratching my neck, face, and stomach. I was aware of the hole in my undershirt and the absence of my client.

"What can I do for you?" I said.

"Ah," said Nelson, enjoying his moment before pouncing. "You could invest a few million dollars in Mirador real estate if you had it, but barring that, you can come for a little ride with me and Alex so we can talk over old times and the scrape you put on my car and Lope Obregon's skull last night."

There was a bowl of water in one corner of the wagon and a mirror over it. I moved the five steps to it, examined the bowl to determine if it was clean, came to no conclusion, and stuck my face into it. It was cold and tight. I dried myself on a towel that was definitely not clean and turned to grin in the mirror. I looked rotten.

"So I'm under arrest," I said, reaching for my jacket, which had gotten kicked around by clowns or cops.

"No, no," chuckled Nelson, advancing on me. He was a few inches shorter than me, and his teeth were clean. His breath smelled minty and sweet enough to make me feel like throwing up.

"Good," I said. "I've got some work to do here. Been good to see you again." I tried to step past him, and he moved out of the way.

"Alex is out there," he said. "He's not going to let you go. I told you never to come back to Mirador. Now I'm going to show you I mean what I say. I really do. If I don't show people I mean what I say, pretty soon people are going to start testing, taking advantage. Can't have that happen."

"So we're going for a little ride?" I guessed.

"Precisely," he said, pointing to the door. "And at the end of that little ride I'm going to watch with great regret while Alex . . ."

"Teaches me that you mean what you say?" I supplied.

"Thank you," he said politely. "I rather expect that it will be a singularly instructive lesson, and I cannot vouch for what remains of your nose."

"Sheriff, did anyone ever tell you that you sweat like a hog?" I whispered.

Nelson's grin dropped for a full half-second and then came back happier than ever.

"We have chatted long enough," he said. "Now let us get to it."

There were no windows I could go through, just the door. I stepped out into the morning. It was foggy, a gray fog that hid the tents and train and anything else not more than fifteen feet away, but it didn't hide the sounds. Motors were churning, people calling, animals bellowing. Laughs, shouts. The spots of light that managed to make their way through the fog were like pinholes that showed nothing beyond themselves. Alex was clear and near in his denims and white cowboy hat. He was bulky and dark, not a beer bulky but a natural bulky, and I knew what he could do. There was no smile on his face, no sign of recognition.

"Good morning, Alex," I said. *"Como está?"*

Now that we were outside and within Alex's reach, Nelson felt safe enough to violate my body. He put a hand on my shoulder and squeezed gently, as if he were a trainer preparing his fighter before the scheduled four-rounder.

"Alex isn't much of a talker, as you may recall," said Nelson. He fit his hat back on his head and played with it quickly to make it feel snug. "Car's over there," he said. "Fog is tempting, but Alex would catch you, and Alex gets mad if he has to run in the morning."

"You still doing Alex's talking for him?" I said. "He's a big boy. Maybe he can tell me how he feels. Maybe Alex doesn't want to march on my face."

Some figures, I couldn't tell how many, were moving toward us through the fog as Alex stepped forward to help guide me to the sheriff's car.

"Alex will do what he must," said Nelson piously. "Is that not right, Alex?"

Alex shrugged. I had no idea what Alex thought about me, whether he liked me, hated me, or didn't give a damn either way. I did know from looking at him that he'd do what Nelson wanted, that times were still hard and money scarce in Mirador.

Nelson and Alex flanked me and moved forward two or three feet before two figures in the fog came in range. One of the figures was Emmett Kelly. The other was a sinewy man with a perfect thin, waxed mustache. He was wearing a gray windbreaker and had a serious look on his lined face. His head was totally bald and looked polished.

"Hold on," said the bald man with Kelly.

"I mean to," said Nelson. "I mean to hold real tight to this rascal. He has committed several crimes and must come to town to deal with his rash acts."

"My name is Elder," said the man with the mustache. "I'm one of the owners of this circus. We hired Mr. Peters last night. He is part of this organization."

"And . . ." grinned Nelson, tightening the grip on my arm.

"And we expect charges to be stated and the employee to be released in good health when those charges are dealt with," said the man. Kelly caught my eye and nodded knowingly. I winked. I didn't know what we were communicating, but it beat being dragged into the fog by the two-man Mirador police force.

"In fact," said Elder, stepping forward, "if the charges are not too grave, we would appreciate dealing with them now. Maybe we can settle this without recourse to a trip to town. We are a bit shorthanded. The war and . . . you understand, I hope."

I think Nelson was about to say that he did not understand when more figures emerged from the fog. It looked like one of those patriotic movies I used to see in grade school with people out of American history stepping through mist to tell me to be a good American and support the war or the President, and they were just as silent as those silent images, but they weren't Presidents. They were a dozen or more men of all ages whose muscles were outlined under their work shirts and jackets.

"I mean to take this man," said Nelson, his voice cracking rather like Jean Alvero, the prostitute of the night before, but there was nothing charming in Nelson's statement, nor was there anything forceful. I looked at Alex, who showed only a twitch of annoyance. There was no backing down in Alex, but he and I and everyone including Nelson could tell that Nelson meant the opposite of what he was saying.

Alex, Nelson, and I were now circled by the circus chorus, and Elder kept getting more and more polite. Nelson's hat came off, and the sheriff found that it needed immediate attention and cleaning with a soggy handkerchief.

"The charges are?" said Elder.

"Assault, disorderly conduct, damage to public vehicle, drunk and disorderly," said Nelson, whose grin was gone.

Elder advanced to within three feet of Nelson and showed an incredibly lined, weatherbeaten face over his mustache. "I'd really like to know who brought the charges."

"A respected member of our community," screeched the sheriff.

"Well," said Elder, looking evenly at Alex and then at the sheriff. "We are shorthanded, and I'm afraid if you take our man here it might mean we couldn't do our show tonight, might have to pack right up and not play our second night in Mirador. Now, I understand some important people in this country plan to bring their kids tonight, you know, take their minds off the war. I think they need a little entertainment, and they'd be awfully damned angry if the circus pulled up and left. They'd like to know who was responsible, and I'm afraid we'd have to tell them about this."

Nelson's eyes went around the circle of faces and came to me. I choked on a smile.

"You wouldn't do that," he said. "You'd lose too damn much money."

"We'd do it," said Elder. "And you'd lose too. You appointed or elected here? Doesn't matter either way."

"Do we take him?" said Alex, looking placidly at Nelson. You could read whatever you wanted or nothing into Alex's face. Nelson might have read disapproval.

"I'm really sorry about last night," I said soberly to Nelson. "I apologize, and I'll pay for the paint job on the police car."

"You step one foot outside this circus ground," Nelson hissed softly in my ear, "and I'll grab your ass so tight you'll need a surgeon to get me loose."

"Colorful," I whispered back.

Alex let go of my arm and walked into the fog in the general direction of town.

"Take two free tickets for tonight," said Elder, handing

the white pieces of cardboard to the sheriff. Nelson snatched them and shoved them in his pocket. Even the chance for a little dignity couldn't deter Nelson from something he could turn into cash.

"I am not an evil or vindictive man, Peters," he said, turning to me. "I'm a man who has a job to do and does it. Mirador has to stay untouched. The people expect that, pay for it, and I mean to give them what they pay for."

"Protection," I said.

"That is right," he said, looking directly into my eyes, and I could see that he meant it. In his own way, he really thought he was a just man on a righteous mission. When was I going to meet a bad guy who knew he was a bad guy? Why did all the bad guys think they were good guys? As he disappeared into the fog, I wondered whether Hitler thought he was a good guy. I was sure he did, and that sudden thought made me feel depressed just when I felt I should have been relieved. I'd just been saved from a beating. I didn't keep count of such things, but it would have been number sixty or seventy, and I would have absorbed it. It was the inability of people to know where they belonged in my fantasy that caused me the real pain.

"Thanks," I said, putting out my hand to Elder, who took it firmly. The circus figures melted back into the fog, and sounds of waking returned.

"The sheriff bluffs awfully easy," he said with a grin that turned his already sun-creased face into a walrus-leather mask. "I'm glad that deputy isn't in charge here, or you'd be on your way to whatever they planned for you."

Light began to penetrate the fog, and I started to see shapes and activity.

"Emmett told me about you," said Elder, looking back at some sound he separated from the noise. "I don't think there's anything going on here, but it's his money if he wants to pay you. I just don't want any panic talk, and I don't want you stirring anything up that isn't there."

A shiny wagon, a massive gold-painted thing, lumbered out into view, pulled by a squat red truck with massive tires.

The truck rumbled past us, drowning out other sounds and our conversation; and I found myself looking into the face of the creature in the cage, the gorilla, whose hands clung to the bars of the jiggling cage and who examined me without curiosity.

Kelly backed away as the cage pulled past.

"Gargantua," he said, without affection. "When I joined Ringling a year ago," he went on, watching the wagon rumble off, "they wanted me to be part of an act with him. It was called The Wedding of Gargantua. Willie, that's my clown, would be the jailer outside the cage, keeping the gorilla from running away before the wedding. I never liked the idea, and the monkey didn't take to me. Went wild. We gave up the idea. I think some clown did him wrong once."

By now the fog was almost gone. I could smell something cooking, and my stomach rumbled.

"Let's take him to chow," said Elder. "Peters, let's just call you an unpaid member of circus security for a few days. You do what you have to, to satisfy Emmett, and then we say good-bye. Fair enough?"

"OK with me," said Kelly, putting a hand to his balding head.

"Right," I added.

"But I tell you there's no secret plot going on here," said Elder. "I've been circusing for . . ."

"Elder," came a scream, and the three of us turned our heads. A woman, her hands in the pocket of a mannish gray jacket, came running forward. She spotted Elder and slowed down to a fast walk. Her dark eyes scanned the three of us, and her mouth was open as if someone had slapped her and she was afraid to say so.

"What is it, Peg?" Elder said.

"Tanucci, the young one," she gasped. "He . . . he took a fall. The doc's with him."

Elder ran off with the woman after him. I looked at Kelly, whose eyes were wide.

"An accident," I said. "Circuses must have accidents all the time."

"Yes," said Kelly. "But most of the accidents happen to the laborers, not the performers."

"OK," I said. "Let's take a look."

Before we could take ten steps after Elder, something happened. Kelly sensed it before I did and stopped. I wasn't sure what it was at first, and then I could tell that the sounds of the circus had changed. The machine sounds had dominated a few minutes ago. Now the sound of animals took over. Bleats and cries and screams and roars, a sad madness of sound.

"What . . ." I started.

"I think Tanucci's dead," said Kelly.

chapter 3

There were four Tanuccis. Five if you counted the one lying dead on the rolled-up canvas in the corner of the tent. The dead Tanucci was dressed like the live ones, in blue tights and a top. His arms were at his sides and his legs together as if he were about to dive into the sky. Just one step forward, a perfect flip of his dark arms and tight, compact body, and he would go soaring into the air and through a hole high above in the big top. But that wasn't going to happen. What might happen was that Tanucci's body would roll from its balanced place on the mat and lose its dignity.

The four remaining Tanuccis were an older man and woman, a young woman, and a teenage boy. The older man and woman held each other's hands and looked at the body. All four of them looked down, as if the dead man held a camera and they had been told to pose solemnly.

It had happened to me before, that nightmare moment when everyone is turned to stone and no one wants to break the spell, even though everyone knows whoever doesn't break it will stay there forever. The next step meant choosing an emotion or letting one out that you maybe didn't know was there.

Or worse, it meant feeling nothing, which soon turned to guilt.

Elder broke through and walked over to the Tanuccis, taking the older man's arm in both of his. "Carlo, I am sorry, truly sorry. What happened?"

The young Tanucci girl turned her head in a daze toward Elder. "The rigging," she said. "The Mechanic tore. Ricco . . . he came down on . . ."

"Rennata is the only one who speaks English," Kelly whispered to me, his voice almost as unsteady as hers.

"Who's the Mechanic?" I whispered back, keeping my eye on the doctor who was examining the body. The doctor was a remarkably old man named Ogle, who looked as if he would probably need help getting up and would surely need help if the body rolled over on him.

"Mechanic's a what, not a who," said Kelly. "The leather safety harness flyers wear in practice sessions. Someone controls it from the ground. They must have been working out something new or having trouble with something old."

At the entrance flap of the tent, a crowd had gathered but was being held back by a trio of men.

"Do accidents happen a lot in the circus?" I said. Elder was going down the line of Tanuccis, consoling them in English they couldn't understand but with a tone they could.

"No, not much," said Kelly. "Sometimes, but usually when it does happen it's because an animal acted like an animal. You know, a lion or a bear smells something, hears something. But it happens."

Peg, the dark-eyed woman with the gray man's jacket who had called Elder to the tent, stayed just a step behind him, trying to see his face to know how she was supposed to act.

"He's dead," said Doc Ogle in a high monotone. It was the tone of my landlady back in Los Angeles, the tone of the deaf who have no idea how loud they are talking and no sense of emotion in the words they can't hear. Everyone else in the tent had known Tanucci was dead the moment they saw him, but the doctor's pronouncement hit behind the knees of the older Tanucci woman, who crumpled forward and would have smashed face first into a metal rigging bar if the older man had not pulled her back and up with a single, powerful pull.

The tent smelled of horse and elephant crap, of straw and stale sweat. For twenty-five dollars a day plus expenses I sometimes had to get a little closer to things beating below the surface than most of us want to get. It always attracted me, that exposed, tender fear. I wanted to touch it in others but was afraid of how it might contaminate me. Grief was as dangerous as disease.

The Tanuccis moved forward toward the body, supporting each other, and Kelly stepped up to help the Tanucci girl, who looked a little unsteady.

"Neck bone and spinal cord just snapped like that," said the doctor, struggling to get up. He wore a dark plaid coat, and his white wild hair had been combed by a drunken witch. He looked more like a clown than Kelly, and his voice cut through the smells and sobs like a set of instructions for building a model airplane.

"Probably not a long fall," he said, addressing himself to everyone assembled. "Probably dead as soon as he hit."

"Thank God," said Peg.

Well, that was one way of looking at it. I knew some who might be a little angry with God for allowing Himself to accept the whim of young Tanucci's death, but maybe God was just an onlooker.

I shook my head. I mean I literally shook my head to try to clear it. Sometimes I get angry and sometimes I get serious. Not often, but sometimes. I almost never get depressed. To get depressed you have to have a long-range plan that fouls up. I don't have any long-range plans. I go job to job, concussion to concussion, dime to dime. If people get in the way of a car or a bullet or one of the grisly weapons including bad luck, I step to the side and keep going, hoping for not much more than the chance to finish up whatever I'm working on.

But the circus got to me. First the dead elephant, and now the Tanuccis. Hell, if I was going to feel guilty, I might as well feel it all the way. I felt worse about the dead elephant than I did about Tanucci. Tanucci picked the circus. He had a chance, maybe had some enemies, maybe didn't check the harness. Maybe . . .

I walked past the small crowd and glanced at the people at the entrance, straining to see in. One or two of them were Cora and Thelma, the Siamese twins. Beyond them, more people were talking, asking questions. The ones in front had heard the doctor and seen the reaction. I moved to the circus ring in the corner and to the trapeze in its center, no more than a dozen feet over the ground. The Mechanic thing Kelly had mentioned dangled down from a pole. It swung slightly in the flat air about six feet over the ground. I didn't even have to touch it to see what I didn't want to see. The place where the leather belt had given way was torn for about one quarter of an inch. The other three inches of the belt were cut. I couldn't tell how thick or tough the leather was or how sharp the knife had been that cut it, but it was clear that the final break in the leather had been jagged and rough and the rest along a straight line.

I was about to touch the harness to be sure when I heard Elder's voice behind me say to either the doctor or the Tanuccis, "We're going to have to call the police."

The word police may have done it. Maybe it was something else, but a small group from the tent entrance broke through, a group of four. Then someone took charge at the entrance and cut off the crowd. The last one through was a short, fat man who waddled forward slowly, far behind. In front of him were a big man wearing a dark gray suit and a dark gray look, a thin man in gray work clothes whose silent tears caught the light against his pale cheeks, and a red-haired young woman in spangled blue tights wearing a little hat with a tall feather.

"Hold it," shouted Elder, stretching out his right hand toward the crowd. "Right there. Stop. No one else in here. No Kinders, no brass. Peters."

I turned and moved to Elder, who whispered, "We've got to get Nelson back here. You want to take the home run. Now's the time."

"Can't," I said, trying to ease him away from the Tanuccis. "Cops don't like it when people they want to nail run away from murder scenes."

It was Elder's turn to move me away from the others by grabbing my jacket and stepping back. His grip could have gone through my arm.

"Hold it," I cried, trying to shake him loose with less success than Billy Conn had had against Joe Louis.

"Look," he said evenly, looking over my shoulder at the small group gathering around the doc, the corpse, and the grieving family. "Don't try to make a profit on this. Don't turn the circus into a . . ."

"Circus?" I finished.

"For a lot of these people," he said, his mustache bobbing up and down, "the only thing they call hometown or a religion or anything is the circus. You make them think murder, and the panic you'll see is like nothing you've ever seen. These are people who put their life on the wire every day and twice on Saturdays and Sundays."

"But it's murder," I repeated. "No doubt. If you let a little circulation back into my arm, I'll show you."

He let loose a little, and I led him toward the harness. My back had been to it, and the small group had gotten between Elder and me and the ring where the Tanuccis had been practicing. No one was watching us as we moved toward the rigging except the fat little man who stood at the edge of the huddled group.

"Who's he?" I asked Elder, who glanced at the man.

"I don't know," Elder said indifferently. "Never saw him. Probably a lot louse, someone from town who hangs around, always wanted to join the circus but let it . . ."

"Gone," I said, stopping when I had a clear view of the rigging.

The rope from which the harness with the severed belt had been hanging was gone. The rope was still swaying above the even cut.

"Someone cut it down," I said, hurrying forward and grab-

bing the rope to make it stop and tell me something. It didn't.
An animal whimper came from the group around the body.
"The belt was cut almost all the way through," I explained.
"The killer . . ."

"Hold it," said Elder, putting his hand to his shiny head.
The possibilities were coming too fast and hard, and he had to
slow things down. I was the thing that had to be slowed. "Harness is gone, right. It is cut down, right. But I can think of some
quick reasons other than a murder cover-up. Some morbid
souvenir hunter could have snatched it. Or maybe one of the
family or a kinker, a performer who has some crazy idea about
burning the offending thing responsible. We got people from all
over the damn world in this circus with all kinds of ideas. There
are enough screwy things going on in a show like this without
this Jackpot."

"Jackpot," I repeated, looking around at the people in the
tent.

"Tall stories about the circus. We have so many of them
that the very idea has a special name."

"Someone in this tent right now cut down that harness,"
I said. "No one else got in here between the time I found the
harness and now. You were talking to me, so that lets you out."

"Thanks," he said sarcastically. "Now what do you plan,
a search of everyone in the tent? A search for the harness?"

"Damn right," I said, "before . . ."

But "before" came. Curiosity overcame restraint and respect. The crowd surged in. I tried to stay near the place where
the harness had been. Whoever took it couldn't have hidden it
far away.

"You better come with me," said Elder.

"But," I protested, "we'll lose the harness."

"You come or I carry you," he said. The short, red-haired
woman bumped into me. She was holding her red sequined cap
on her head. Its ostrich feather threatened to tickle God. Well,
maybe He could do with a good laugh.

Working against the crowd, with Elder ignoring questions
put to him by people of all sizes, accents, ilks, and colors, we

made it into the near sunlight. The fog was almost gone, and the sun burned gray.

"Office," he said, guiding me.

"Wait," came a voice from behind, Kelly's voice.

We didn't wait, but he had caught up by the time we reached a circus railroad car that said "Office" on it. Elder followed me into the little space with a desk in the middle and a cot in the corner and motioned me to one of the three wooden chairs. I sat, and so did Kelly. Elder didn't. He leaned against the steel wall of the office wagon, touched his fine mustaches to be sure they were still there and not drooping, folded his arms and glared at me.

"Murder," I repeated.

I could sense Kelly sagging next to me. Elder said nothing. I looked into his eyes and saw something I hadn't seen before and knew what he was going to say before he said it. I felt like speaking along with him, but the thought was just enough behind to keep it from happening.

"Know how old I am, Peters?" he said. "Sixty-two. I've seen 'em torn up, and I've seen a few murders. Not with this circus, but others. I've even helped cover them up. The circus is its own world. It's a moving world that only stops a few days in the world of someone else. You understand what I'm saying? Even if there was a murder, there wasn't any murder."

The walls of the office were covered with old posters with faded pictures of clowns and girls in tights. The word "circus" stood out in every one, gaudy, proud. Mills, Sells and Floto; Mix; Cole. I looked at the posters and heard Elder out.

"Maybe that's something the management has to decide," I said.

"Maybe," he said, arms still folded and looking at Kelly, who had brought this Los Angeles outsider into the circus. "But I have no evidence of a murder, and I have no intention of . . ."

"I believe him," said Kelly softly.

"Look, Emmett," said Elder, pushing himself away from the wall and pointing a finger at Kelly.

"Tom," said Kelly with a sad smile, "you believe it too."

Elder's accusing, attacking finger stopped in midair, and his hand moved to his face. Elder's eyes closed and looked tired and wrinkled. He rubbed them.

"The elephants, Tom," said Kelly softly.

One more drop in the decibel level, and I wouldn't be able to hear either one of them. I had the feeling they could communicate without words anyway. I had the feeling that I didn't belong in this world, couldn't wisecrack my way through it like the bars, cracked streets, movie studios, and damp office buildings I was familiar with. I wanted to get up and leave.

"Someone tried to do me, Tom," Kelly said. "I told you. Peters is just . . ."

Elder's free hand came up with palm out to stop Kelly. His other hand covered weary eyes that didn't want to see, but they had to. He put both hands at his sides and looked at me, having some difficulty focusing.

"Not saying you're right or wrong, what do we do next?"

"You saw the Mirador police," I said. "I've seen them trying to nail a killer. They nab the closest foreigner and call it a day. With the people you have here, Nelson will have the case wrapped up in an hour. Of course, he'll have the wrong killer, probably someone who can't speak English well enough to defend himself. Suggestion. Call Nelson back. Let him come to his own conclusion which, without our shoving the truth under his nose, will be that it was an accident. Meanwhile, we try to find the killer and turn him over to Nelson with something real to go on."

Something warm and sweet-smelling passed the wagon and came in under the door, reminding me how much alive I was and making me suddenly and insanely hungry.

"Well?" I pushed.

"How?"

"I go through everyone in that tent," I explained. "I find out how many have something against the circus, how many . . . like that. If we're lucky, I get it down to one or two or three, and we turn them over. Go through their things, try to find some evidence. Hell, maybe we push them around or tell them lies."

Elder sighed and looked out the window. "OK, let's give it a day or two and hope the killer, if there is one, has had enough. But keep it quiet."

"With everything that goes on here, that might just be possible," I said.

Elder laughed, one of those it's-not-funny-but-what-else-can-you-do-to-me laughs. "You don't understand the circus, Peters. You piss behind the calliope at three A.M. on a moonless night, and by morning you'll have five questions at breakfast about your kidneys. Give it a try, give it a try. What do you need?"

"Breakfast," I said, and breakfast it was.

Five minutes later, Kelly and I were seated together in a mess tent. The death of Tanucci had circled Kelly in a cone of silence which he had trouble breaking out of. It didn't, however, affect his appetite. We were breakfast stragglers, sitting as far away from the kitchen as we could get. Our eggs, ham, and coffee were accompanied by the music of clanging spoons, metal plates, running water, and chattering cooks. I didn't need to hear the words. They were talking about death. There is a tone of it that doesn't need words.

"What happens to the circus when there's an accident like this?" I said, trying to ignore the coffee I had just spilt on my shirt. Maybe I could button my top jacket button and hide it.

Kelly shrugged, stopped eating, and tried to look through the wall in the general direction of Tanucci's body.

"We do the show," he said. "Even the Flying Tanuccis. They just do less of an act. Maybe they even mention what happened. Maybe they don't. We don't close up shop. Can't. A circus, especially a shoestring one like this, can't take too many nights down."

He went back to his eggs, and I tried drinking my coffee carefully in a thick white porcelain cup that felt good against my palms.

"And you have to be funny," I said more than asked.

Something like a chuckle came out of Kelly. "You know," he said. "I usually am funnier when I'm down. The towners can't tell. You know the story about Joey Grimaldi? First big circus clown about a hundred years ago. We're still called Joeys because of him. One day his circus is playing Vienna, and Joey is so down he's thinking of quitting. So he goes to a doctor's office he spots on the way to his hotel and tells the doc that he's so depressed that he's thinking of taking his life.

" 'Don't worry,' says the doctor. 'I know just the thing to make you feel better, better enough to keep going. The circus is in town. Just go down there tonight and keep your eyes on Grimaldi the clown, and you'll find yourself laughing.' "

"Nice story," I said, looking across the tent to watch the woman named Peg hurrying toward us.

"Maybe," said Kelly, reaching for another pancake, "but I don't believe it, a Jackpot for clowns. There aren't many suicides in circuses. Circus people seldom give up hope. We learn to live on hope. That's what we talk about most of the time: next year, the next job, things getting better, homes we're going to buy, places we're going to visit, things we're going to be."

"What are you going to be when you grow up?" I said with my crooked smile.

"I used to think I was going to be a cartoonist. I was pretty good. The clown I do, Willie, I really drew him first for an ad agency I worked for back in Kansas City. Then I thought for a while I'd be a trapeze star, center-ring stuff. Was too for a while, did a teeth-hanging act. Damned hard on the jaws. Until a few months back I thought I might like to be in movies, but . . . If I ever grow up, I think I'll just be a clown."

Peg was standing next to us with something in her hand. Her hair was gradually escaping from the hairpins, which tried to hold it against the wind. She was the kind of woman who left a trail of hairpins you could follow to the far reaches of Alaska.

"Hi, Peg," said Kelly. "Want some coffee?"

"No . . . yes . . . I think no," she said, patting back some hair. "Tom said I should give this to you."

I took the sheet of paper from her hand and looked down at the list. It had the names of everyone in the tent when the harness was removed. It included the name of Emmett Leo Kelly and was, as for each person on the list except for me and the final name, followed by a place of birth and a date. Kelly's was Sedan, Kansas, December 9, 1898.

Peg couldn't make up her mind about staying or sitting. I pointed to the bench next to me, and she sat.

"Sheriff is here," she said.

"And . . ." I prodded.

"I think he's convinced it's an accident," she said, reaching for a piece of toast on my plate, realizing what she was doing and pulling her hand back. I took the toast and placed it on the table in front of her.

"I haven't had a chance to eat," she explained, picking up the toast with a guilty hand.

"Your not eating doesn't help the Tanuccis," said Kelly, pouring her a cup of coffee.

She took it, and I discovered that . . .

. . . Dr. Patrick Y. Ogle had been born in Singapore Falls, Maine, eighty years earlier . . .

. . . the Tanuccis were from Corsica . . .

. . . one person in the tent at the time of the theft was a snake charmer named Agnes Sudds . . .

. . . one person was a local businessman from Mirador named Thomas Paul . . .

. . . and one person was a movie director named Alfred Hitchcock.

One of them was probably the murderer. I showed the list to Kelly.

"Can't help you much," he said. "I've only been with this circus a few weeks." He handed the list to Peg, who was consuming whatever Kelly and I weren't holding onto.

"No," said Peg.

"My money's on one of the outsiders," said Kelly. "Probably that Hitchcock fella."

Which, I thought, is why you are a clown and I am a

detective, though there were those who would argue that I would make a better clown than a detective.

"OK," I said, standing up. "Then let's start with Hitch-cock."

chapter 4

He was a short, fat man with a lower lip like a pouting tailor, hair sparse but neatly in place, and wearing a dark suit and tie that looked as if they had just been handed to him by Belman's Cleaning and Dyeing in Hollywood. He was seated in Elder's office with his hands folded on his lap like a schoolboy.

"Hitchcock?" I said.

"I am Alfred Hitchcock," he replied, looking at me with large eyes hooded by lids which suggested indifference, but the eyes gave too much away. "Are you a policeman?"

The word "policeman" seemed to come hard for him. I'd never seen Hitchcock before, but I knew who he was.

"*Suspicion,*" I said.

He looked frightened. His knuckles went white, and his hands remained clasped.

"Of what?" he said.

"No," I smiled. "I've seen *Suspicion.* I've seen your movies. What are you doing here, at the circus?"

"At the moment," he said very slowly with a distinct English accent, "I am being very frightened. Before that I was trying to get some material for a sequence in a film I'm considering."

"A circus scene?"

"Precisely," he said with a slight uplifting of the right side of his mouth that represented pain or an attempt to be friendly. "I'm staying with an acquaintance nearby, and my plan was to stop by for a few hours this morning, get some sense of atmosphere, and present my ideas to the writer. Why have I been asked to talk to you, and who are you?"

I sat on Elder's cot. "Between us, I'm a private investigator. Name is Toby Peters. I'm pretty sure that aerialist Tanucci was murdered."

Hitchcock's eyes opened with interest, and he shifted his fat body slowly to face me. "Murdered," he repeated, either savoring the word or trying to hear it come from his own mouth when it was about something real. "You are sure?" he said.

"As sure as I am that I'd marry Joan Fontaine if she'd have me," I answered. He definitely smiled this time.

"This is better than I could have hoped," he said as much to himself as to me. "But I'm sorry. A man has been murdered, and all I can think of is my movie."

"That's all right," I said, wanting to lie back on the cot but unable to do so with the rigid, rotund director seated across from me. "You're not a suspect. You're more in the way of a possible witness. I saw you come in the tent earlier, and I saw you watching me when I walked over to the practice hitch."

"Yes," he said. "It struck me as rather peculiar that someone should be walking away from the flow of the crowd, the movement toward death. It struck me as an interesting image, the isolation of one man moving away from where the world is looking."

"Did you see anyone go over to that harness, that thing I was looking at, maybe take it down?"

Hitchcock pursed his lips, blinked his eyes, and nodded once. "Someone did, I believe. I wasn't watching really, but I had the sense of a person in blue, rather tall, or something about the person seeming tall."

"Man, woman?" I tried.

"A man-woman," he mused. "No, I don't think so. I should surely have noticed that."

I couldn't tell if he was joking, but he must have been. What I surely couldn't decide was whether the joke was on me or a private entertainment.

"I'm sorry," he said. "I react rather badly when disaster strikes anywhere but on a studio set."

"I forgive you," I said, wondering how to get out of this polite, droll conversation and get murder back to the people where it seemed to belong. "Tall figure, blue?"

"Correct," he nodded, looking at the posters. "I never realized how frightening a circus could be." Instead of looking frightened, he looked quite pleased. "Do you think it would be all right if I stayed today and possibly tomorrow? My friend lives in Mirador. He drove me over this morning."

"I guess so," I said, giving up and lying down on the cot. "I suggest you stay away from the Mirador police."

Hitchcock rose slowly with a distinct grunt. He looked even fatter standing than he did sitting.

"As I have indicated," he said, "I have a morbid fear of the police, dating back to my childhood days when my father had a policeman put me in jail for an hour to teach me what happens to bad boys. I have endeavored since that moment to be a good boy and stay away from policemen."

"I'll run off copies of that philosophy and send it to a few hundred friends of mine who could use it."

"Good afternoon," Hitchcock said politely, moving to the door.

"If you remember anything more about who was standing near that harness, let me know," I said, closing my eyes. "I'll be around."

"I shall," he said and left the wagon.

Thomas Paul, the "businessman" from Mirador, was the next person ushered into the wagon-office by Peg. When I heard the door open I sat up, and it's a good thing I did.

I hadn't had a good look at the man in the business suit

who had run into the tent an hour earlier. I knew he was big, but his face had been covered by a hat. That hat was still on, but it couldn't hide the scar on his face, a purple scar that split his face in half. The right side was sharp-eyed and smiling with a secret joke. The left side was pulled down, distorted by what seemed pain or sorrow. He was a Janus who couldn't be read, happy and sad at the same time. The scar cut across the corner of his mouth, so his speech was slightly distorted.

Grotesqueness was no sign of guilt, just of fascination. I shook his hand and pointed to the chair. He took it. With some stretch of the imagination, his suit might be taken for blue, but it was more black than blue. Paul didn't seem a good bet for a killer. Whoever did it was probably tied in to the death of the elephants for the past few years and was affiliated with the circus.

"Why have I been asked to come in here?" he said, his voice slurred.

"Won't take a minute," I said reassuringly, trying to make up my mind if it would be more polite to avoid looking at him or to force myself to keep my eyes on him.

"My visage makes you uncomfortable, Mr. . . ."

"Peters," I said. "I'm sorry."

"I assure you that it is an even greater source of discomfort to me," he said, the one side of his face amused, the other even more in agony from its opposite grin. "War accident. The Ardennes. Shell exploded. I have a feeling that even more will suffer in our current confrontation with the Huns."

"We don't call them Huns anymore," I said. "Nazis."

"It is your war," he said, sitting back. "Call them what you like."

"This is a routine investigation for the insurance company," I said, not liking Mr. Paul. "May I ask you a few questions?"

"You may ask," he said, his eyes never leaving me. "I will decide whether or not I wish to answer."

I found a pencil and began to doodle on a sheet of paper on Elder's desk. I drew cubes tied together and worked on

Koko the clown. I didn't care if Paul knew I wasn't taking notes. "How long have you lived in Mirador?" I asked.

"Four years," he said. "Though I fail to see how such information could help the insurance company."

"Simply trying to fill out the form," I said. "Background information establishes the credibility of the witness."

"I witnessed nothing," he said. "The accident had already taken place when I arrived."

"What were you doing here, at the circus?" I tried.

"I am a reasonably wealthy man," he said. "Primarily real estate in various parts of the nation. I have some plans for revitalizing Mirador and the county. Hope to draw business interests here."

"To help the county while you sell land?"

"It is mutually advantageous," he agreed. "I have no intention of defending my interest in making money. It is my interest, my passion. I came here today to try to begin negotiations to have the circus set up a permanent West Coast headquarters here. Just a preliminary step. The idea would be to make the circus management welcome, to plant the seed."

"Your sheriff didn't exactly make them welcome this morning," I said amiably.

"Mr. Nelson is sometimes a bit overzealous," said Paul. "But he knows his responsibility."

"And he knows who pays the rent," I added, looking up. That face betrayed nothing because it displayed everything. "Mr. . . ."

"Peters," I said.

"I am not here to engage in argument with you. I wish to cooperate with the circus if I can, for reasons which I have now made quite clear to you. I will make it clear to the management of this circus that it is to their advantage to have a location like Mirador where the government, which includes the sheriff, fully understands the plans and needs of the business community."

"As long as the circus stays on the good side of the business community," I said.

"I don't know where you got your training, nor in what," he said. "It certainly wasn't in business or economics."

"Tanucci fell from a harness while rehearsing," I said. "Did you see the harness hanging in the ring over to the right side of the tent?"

"I do not know. I do not remember. What difference does it make?"

"None, Mr. Paul," I said, standing up. "I'm just doing my job."

He stood up. Physically, he looked like a larger version of Alfred Hitchcock, but there was something tight about him. Maybe it was just his twisted face or the fact of having seen a dead man and being asked questions about it. I wasn't feeling any too loose myself. But I had a job, so I moved one step up the ladder to a broken friendship.

"What do you think about circuses, Mr. Paul?"

"Very little," he said. "They are businesses which can occupy space and bring jobs, which means more people who need more land. It seems a bit unsavory, but that doesn't bother me. Carelessness bothers me."

His eyes, both the good and bad one, took me in, from graying hair to scuffed shoes, pausing, I was sure, at my coffee stain.

"I try not to let it bother me," I said. "Like rude people. If they feel better making enemies instead of friends, it's their back that has to be watched. People like that hire people like me. So if you ever need a private detective . . ."

"I should look you up," he finished.

"No," I said. "Go to San Diego. There are two private eyes named Maling and Markham who take hopeless cases. Some people will do anything for a buck."

"Times are hard," said Paul. I caught no irony in his words.

"They're always hard," I said.

"I'm amazed," he said, opening the door. "We actually agree on something."

When he left, the room grew larger, and I breathed deeply.

Then the room got smaller again, and I wondered if I had reacted to the way he looked or if he had really brought the tension in, in some other form than his face.

Agnes Sudds came next, and a welcome change she was, a breath of cold simplicity in a room full of hot air. She was small, red of hair, with a face that people surely called pert and a blue twinkling dress which showed a lot of Sudds. Her hand remained on the tiny hat with the tall feather that threatened to fall off.

"Why don't you just take it off?" I said as she ducked to make it through the door.

"You ain't even Boss Canvas Man," she said sharply. "And someone should have told you I take it off for nobody, especially a First of May like you." With that, she sat and crossed her legs.

"I meant your hat, not your britches, and what's a First of May?" I moved out from behind the desk and leaned against it to look down at her.

"A newcomer to the circus," she said. I could see now that she had gum in her mouth.

"You like Glenda Farrell?" I said.

She shrugged.

"Ginger Rogers?"

She lit up. "I can dance like that," she said. "I can sing too. I know a guy who knows a producer."

"So do I," I said.

"Mine's real," she said.

"Maybe we can discuss mine," I said, leaning toward her.

Then she took off her blue cap and put it on the floor next to her. I saw why she had been holding it down. A small green snake perched on her head and looked around the room. I didn't turn to stone, but I did head back behind the desk.

"There's a snake on your head," I said, looking for a weapon and wondering how I could kill the snake without destroying the potential victim.

"Of course," she sighed with exasperation. "I work snakes. Abdul is little, but he's full of poison. I work the big snakes too.

Rattlers, small boa, python, even. That's for show. Abdul is the real thing. He gets his fangs in you, you're dead in maybe, I don't know, the time it takes to get to the toy in Cracker Jacks."

"You always carry him around with you?" I said, watching Abdul watch me.

"No, but I wanted to show him to you," she said seriously. "Elder said this was about what happened this morning. I . . . I did it."

"You did it?" I said.

"Right," she agreed, popping her gum. The pop scared the hell out of Abdul, who curled back on her head.

"The Tanucci kid Marco was after me for weeks. I told him no chance. Well, that's what I told him. I didn't want that wife of his, Rennata, after me, but he was a cute kid and if he had stayed with it . . . but I told him no yesterday and showed him Abdul. I think he was a little upset this morning. Maybe because of me and Abdul. I mean, if a guy really wants you, he's not going to let a snake or a 'no' end it, right?"

"Right," I agreed, having just decided that I didn't really want Agnes Sudds.

"So maybe he had me and Abdul on his mind this morning and took a fall," she said, reaching up to her head. I held my breath. Abdul pulled back as if to strike. She held up a finger, made a circle with it, and reached back quickly to grab the snake neatly right behind his head. She pulled him down to her lap and stroked him carefully.

Agnes smiled and snapped her gum again. "Trick," she said. "I could see him in the window behind you. Like a mirror."

I had nothing to say.

"So we did it," she said.

Some moisture came back into my mouth. But so did the acrid taste of part of my breakfast.

"Don't be too hard on yourself, Agnes," I said. "I'm sure you and Abdul had nothing to do with Mr. Tanucci's death."

"I'm not being hard," she said. "Trial might be good for

my career. You know. Circus star drives aerialist to death when she spurns his love. That sort of thing."

"I'm sorry," I said, trying to think of a way to get her to the door without getting too close.

"Can't we make some kind of deal?" she said, holding up Abdul. "I mean, you guys turn me in to the cops and call the radio stations and the newspapers. Maybe I did it. You can't be sure."

"Right," I said, "I can't be sure, but . . ."

"I would be very grateful," she said, removing her gum with her free hand and dropping it into Elder's wastebasket. She turned her even-toothed smile at me. Ginger Rogers with a snake. Toby Peters was nowhere near Eden and not tempted.

"Let me think about it," I said softly, looking into her green eyes. "I'll get back to you later."

There were about thirty seconds of silence while she poised and only gradually got the idea.

"I've got my own wagon," she said. "Behind the big top. Green wagon near the end."

I could see why Agnes had her own wagon. "I'll remember," I said. "I really will."

Then Agnes and Abdul left. Peg came in almost immediately after, bearing a cup of coffee in the white circus mug. It was full of sugar and almost half-cream, which was just the way I like it.

"Thanks," I said, taking it from her hands. Her hair was almost all down now and looking better with each battle lost against the army of pins. Our hands touched.

"I thought you might be needing this after Agnes," she said.

"You might have warned me," I said.

"I wasn't sure you'd believe me," she said with a small smile.

I leaned back and looked at the posters while I drank. Then I looked out the window and watched an elephant walk by. I found myself dreaming of what it would be like to have a real office instead of a closet behind a dentist's office.

"Peg," I said. "Did you murder Tanucci?"

"No," she said.

"Good," I sighed, putting my feet on the desk and looking into the brown coffee.

"And you just believe me?" she asked.

"I don't know. I guess I don't want anyone who would bring me coffee and sympathy and sanity to be a killer. Sure you're not the killer?"

"Positive," she said.

"That's a relief," I said with a grin.

She laughed, a nice laugh.

"You're maybe thirty," I said. "Too shy to be a performer. Maybe you had a little college. Dull small-town life. Circus looked good, so you got up the nerve to ask for a job. Elder needed someone, and you fell in love with him."

She was looking down and biting her lower lip. "Something like that," she said softly. "For some people it's movies or fairy tales. I didn't start dreaming till I was about twenty-five, and I found the circus." She looked up at me with a grin that could have turned to a cry. "I'll grow up someday," she said. It sounded like a promise to some daddy or teacher way beyond the me she was talking to.

"Forget it," I said, draining the last of the coffee and looking at the few grains at the bottom of the cup. "I never grew up. Have no plans to. Took me almost forty years to find that out. I lost my wife when we both finally agreed on that, and I've been playing private detective ever since."

She brightened, and I could see that her eyes were brown and wide. "And you've had fun?"

"It beats growing up," I said. "You are a pretty girl."

"No, I'm all right, and I'm not a girl. You don't talk like you look."

"I look like a reheated meatball because my brother played a tune on my face once too often and because not growing up can get you in trouble."

I'm not sure where we were going, but I didn't get a chance

to find out. Elder came through the door. He looked at me. Then he looked at Peg. He seemed more relieved than upset by what he saw. My guess was that he would have been happy for Peg to pin her fairy tale on someone else.

"Problem, Peters," he said.

We had gone almost two hours without an attack on a clown, elephant, or trapeze artist.

"Rennata Tanucci is missing," said Elder.

"So," I said. "This is a big circus. Maybe she's just getting some sympathy from someone, or she went for a walk."

"Maybe," he agreed, "but why did she take an elephant with her?"

chapter 5

The Tanucci clan shared a train wagon. It was divided into three compartments, each a tiny room. We—Elder, I, and the three Tanuccis—crowded into one of the compartments, sitting on the lower of two bunk beds and standing in the corners. The family had changed into costume for the afternoon performance. Each was dressed in blue tights with white fluffy trimming and a white cape. I had the feeling I was questioning the Marvel family. I wanted to know what they thought had happened to Rennata, to the elephant, to Marco. I wanted to let them know I was sorry and that I wanted to help. It would have been easier if they spoke some English or I knew some Italian. Elder was no help.

"Why did she go?" I shouted. Shouting always stimulates those who cannot understand to grope through a foreign language. It forces the words to the center of the being and translates them. Only this time it didn't work. Actually, it never works.

The older man, Carlo, tilted his chin up and looked at me. His head was heavy with moist, thick black hair that suggested a dye job. His face was thick and brown and lined, a worn face that belonged in a Camel ad in *Look* magazine. He turned to the other members of his family and said, *"Qui?"*

They gave him some advice. He agreed and shook his head. "No," he said with great dignity and no relation to my question.

"Rennata or the kid did all the translating," said Elder. "This isn't going to get us anywhere."

"You mean no one else in this circus speaks Italian?" I asked.

"Sure, but these people aren't exactly full of trust," he explained. "They've been getting some hard talk in some of the towns we've hit. A couple of times people have even called Carlo Mussolini during the act. He damned near dropped Tino one time. The way Rennata told it, they had to run from Italy with a small carnival. Carlo's brother was a secretary or something in the Italian Communist party. The brother was bumped off, and Carlo was afraid for his family and got out. He has more reason to hate the Fascists than the audience does, but go figure out towners."

Elder and Carlo had been looking at each other in understanding through the explanation, and Carlo had clearly picked up enough words like "Mussolini" and "Communist" to figure out what was happening.

"Does he know that the kid might have been murdered?" I asked Elder.

"He knows," came a voice, but it wasn't Elder's. It was the now youngest Tanucci, Tino.

Carlo said something quickly and earnestly to the boy. The mother put a hand on his arm, and Tino touched her reassuringly.

"My English," he said, "is not so very good, but is enough. Rennata told us that Marco was maybe morted, murdered."

He was a short figure, the darkest of the clan, with straight black hair down his neck. He was somewhere in his late teens, but I couldn't tell where. His forehead was creased with the strain of publicly speaking English, a task he had probably not planned to take on for some time.

"What did she say?"

"She say she saw something, someone, and someone saw her seeing this," he said. "It was not so clear to me, something to do with our equip . . . I don't know how you say this word."

"Equipment," I supplied. "She saw someone messing with your equipment before your brother fell. Is that it?"

"*Sí,*" he agreed. "She saw."

"Who was it?" I pushed.

The young man shook his head. "I no know. She say she would take care. She was a very mad." He showed mad by shaking his head furiously. "She say she . . . That's all."

One simple conclusion was that Rennata Tanucci had seen whoever cut the harness or whoever had taken it down after the murder. She was now going to find that person and do something to him or her involving an elephant. The number of unpleasant things someone could do with a two-ton elephant did not elude me or Elder.

"She's crazy enough," Elder confirmed, touching his lower lip.

"It can't be that easy to hide an elephant," I said.

The Tanuccis listened to what they couldn't understand, and the young man tried to translate for them.

"Did anyone hate your brother, have a fight with your brother before this morning?" I asked. "Was anything on his mind?"

"Yes," said the young man. "Marco say, said, he saw someone in the elephant tent. Saw him when circus up go do something. Then elephant go fried. Marco said maybe it not accident. Now, maybe . . ."

"Maybe," I finished, "someone killed Marco because he saw them setting up the rigging to kill the elephant. Then Rennata saw the same person fooling with your equipment and figured she had a murderer. It makes sense."

"The elephant," sighed Elder.

"Thanks," I said to the Tanuccis, taking each of their hands. "We'll find Rennata and bring her back."

"*Gracia,*" said the mother, a firm blonde with enough

makeup to show she was hiding her face and feelings. Elder and I backed out of the wagon, and the trio didn't move.

Outside the wagon, we looked beyond the circus grounds for a two-ton elephant and saw nothing.

"As Charlie Chan would say, 'Two-ton elephant must leave deep tracks in mud.' "

Elder nodded in agreement. "Right to the road down there, but two tons isn't enough to make holes in asphalt and rock."

The road was the one I had come down to find the circus. It led down to the highway going one way and off into the farmlands in the other.

"I'll head for town," I said. "You take some people the other way."

"Doesn't make sense," said Elder sensibly. "Nelson finds you in Mirador and you might not come out."

"Right, but I know the town better than you and how to stay away from him."

"That's a lousy argument," said Elder, pulling his jacket over his neck. The afternoon was cool, but not cold. The sky had clouded over and promised something damp. My back twinged, and I looked at my watch. I hadn't any reason to know the time before this, and my watch didn't help much. It was my one inheritance from my father, if you don't count the debts on his Glendale grocery store. The watch stopped when it wanted to, started when it wanted to, and showed a hell of a lot more independence than my old man ever did, which may have been why I kept it. My old man's indecision was probably a major contribution to my brother Phil's becoming an angry cop and my seeking out violence.

Whatever the reason, my watch said it was two o'clock.

"What time is it?" I asked Elder. We stepped out of the mud rut to let some bears walk by, led by a man who looked almost as much like a bear as the bears. The bears, in fact, were dressed better than the man, in blue tutus. They would be cute from the audience. The audience wouldn't have found them so cute this close up. Bears definitely do not brush their teeth.

"Lotze," grunted the man who looked like a bear, when one of the bears hesitated and decided to growl in my face. Elder ignored the whole thing and bit his lower lip.

"I don't like it," he said.

"I don't either, but we have no choice," I answered.

"You, Peters, are a liar," grinned Elder, a wise grin I didn't care for. My ex-wife had a grin like that. "You do like it. You're as happy as a seal in a fish house."

I shrugged. He was right. There are some people who run from trouble and call it evil, and others who exist for games and thrills. There are some people who tell you boxing matches are savage and others like me who simply like to watch two guys fight. The big dangers you don't set yourself up for, don't have a choice about, like war, they aren't fun. It has something to do with making the decisions or having them made for me. I was going into Mirador. I never claimed I was smart. I'm more a bull terrier than a fox.

"If either of us isn't back in one hour," I suggested, "someone from the circus should go for the state police. There's a state police headquarters about twelve miles south on the Pacific Coast highway."

"Right," said Elder. "There's no point in telling you to be careful. You have no intention of being careful."

"I'll be careful," I said, and I really meant to be.

Ten minutes later, with a thin drizzle hitting my windshield, I headed toward Mirador while I listened to Hop Harrigan. After the announcer told us how to spot Nazi planes, Hop had to deal with two Japanese who had taken his plane and planned to do a suicide run at a dam.

There was no elephant on the main street of Mirador. The drizzle had sent humans inside too. I drove down one of the streets off the town circle. Mirador wasn't too big, but it did sprawl around. I drove down the familiar road, where Howard Hughes had rented a house in which a murder had taken place, and past the Gurstwald estate, where the murderer had come from. No elephants. I drove around hills and roads for another twenty minutes till I started to worry about my gas and went back toward town along the beach road.

I almost missed it. If the rain had been a little heavier and darker, I would have. I stopped the car, got out and listened to the light drops ping off my head, and looked at the elephant tracks in the sand.

I had switched to my rumpled gabardine windbreaker, a May Company special whose zipper had been destroyed by my two-year-old niece Lucy. The rain pittered a warning to my trick back, but I couldn't stop.

My .38 was in the car, but I didn't think a .38 would stop an elephant. It might make him good and mad, but it wouldn't stop him. It wasn't really the elephant I was worried about.

The tracks were clear, not too deep but clear, and I followed them along the shore and around a bend in the rocks, where I found myself looking up at the lost hope of the county, the hidden ambition of the town, the unfinished hotel and recreation spa inhabited now by softly cooing gulls and one or two loudly cawing crows. No elephant.

"Rennata," I called. "My name is Peters. Elder sent me."

I thought I heard something, a shuffling, breathing sound behind one of the creaking boards of a building. Around the corner I went and found myself eye to knee with the elephant. His eyes, red and frightened, were a good four feet above me.

What do you say to an elephant on the beach?

"Hi," I tried. "How've you been?"

The elephant took a step back from me, a lumbering step, and waved its trunk. Beyond him on the sand I could see a heap of cloth which might or might not contain a human form. I pushed my back against the rusted steel side of a building next to the elephant and began to ease my way past, saying soothing things like, "Good boy," and "Easy, big fella."

I had just decided to try a lullaby when hell tore lose. My pushing against the steel siding had given it all it needed to declare its freedom from the single old bolt that held it. The sheet came loose with a screech and clattered against a pillar.

The elephant bellowed, raised one massive right front foot or paw or hoof or whatever it's called, and threw a wild jab in my general direction. I tripped backward as the elephant kicked a steel beam inches from my head and started a clanging that echoed out to sea.

The elephant took another step toward me, and I scrambled back into the rubble, ignoring bruises and bumps. I backed into a corner as the gray hulk moved forward, shaking the long unfinished floor. His weight swayed the warped wood, and I grabbed a glassless window ledge and started to scramble out. The elephant came right after me as I rolled on the sand and looked back over my shoulder. He crashed right through the side of the house, sending out a shower of shrapnel the Big Red One would have backed away from. I didn't know how fast an elephant could run, but I didn't think I could outrun one. On the other hand, I didn't think I had much choice. I went down the beach, and he came bellowing after me.

I wasn't in bad shape. Oh, I'd cut back on the number of days I played handball at the Y on Hope Street back in Los Angeles, but I'd been doing some running and lifting. Fear helped a lot too. I beat the elephant to my car by about four steps, scrambled inside, and went for my glove compartment. The compartment was open, and the gun was gone. The gun was gone, and my Buick was rocking. An elephant was trying to shake me out. A foot thudded against the door at my side, and I could see the dent stop just short of my leg. I put the key in the ignition, turned it on, and gunned the motor. The elephant backed off with a roar that would have frightened Kong. But something had him going, and he came at me again. He stood bellowing a challenge in the drizzle, elephant against car. I knew the car wouldn't survive a battle, and I didn't want to kill an elephant if I didn't have to. So I hit my horn. The first blast startled him. The second blast sent fear into his already blazing eyes. The third, followed by my backing up, sent him running down the beach in the general direction of I-don't-know-where but the opposite direction from where I knew I had to go.

I watched the gray lump disappear and wondered what people would think when they saw the creature racing in the general direction of Mexico. I wondered even more what Arnie the no-neck mechanic would respond when I showed him my door and told him it had been kicked in by a wild elephant.

I drove down the road as close as I could get to where the ghost town stood and the heap of clothing lay. Then I made my way down to the spot, with a good idea of what I would find. There were no footprints around the body except those of the victim herself. I could see it was Rennata Tanucci, knew it was before I pulled back the coat crumpled over her face.

The bullet holes, two of them, were easy to find, one in the middle of her chest, the other in her stomach. I knelt next to her body and followed her hand that seemed to be pointing to something in the sand. The something was a crude drawing that she had apparently made. It looked like a snowman next to a snowman. One snowman was bigger than the other, and the bigger one had two eyes, a hole for a nose, and a mouth that drooped crazily. Both figures were inside a crude box, which may have been a house. It's hard to apply rules of taste to the last creation of a dying artist. The message, whatever it might mean, was shallow and almost worn away by the rain. Her head was turned toward the shore, and her open eyes looked at a brick house on the far ridge above the beach.

"Lady," I said softly, covering her again, "I wonder what the hell you were trying to tell us."

"No doubt," came a voice from behind, "that she expired with the hope that we would catch you. In which case, I am pleased to report, we have achieved that end."

I didn't turn to Nelson's voice right away. There was something I wanted to see first, and I saw it, my .38, about a dozen feet from the body where someone had thrown it.

"You can't expect to go chasing elephants and shooting people on beaches without attracting some attention," said Nelson with clear satisfaction.

I turned and stood up. Nelson and Alex were facing me. Nelson had his gun out. Alex didn't.

"Murder, as you know, is a rare thing in Mirador, Mr. Peters, a rare thing indeed. It is my belief, however, that if it does come, it is good if it is done by an outsider and good if I catch that outsider and even better if it takes place shortly before a major election."

"Then I've done you a favor," I said.

He nodded with a self-satisfied smile. "You might, indeed, say that," he said. "Now, if you would be so good as to step a few feet away from the body of that unfortunate woman, Alex will get that weapon, which, I assume, is yours."

I stepped away slowly. Nelson might take it into his head to simplify matters by gunning down his murderer in a rousing battle. The thought entered his mind as if by telepathy, and he glanced at Alex, who clearly wasn't having any.

"The conscience and strength of my deputy are an inspiration to us all," Nelson said sarcastically, as Alex moved forward to get the .38 in the sand. "You need not bother about handling the weapon, Alex. With this drizzle and sand, fingerprints are unlikely and, certainly in this case, unnecessary."

"Nelson, I didn't kill this woman."

"We shall see," he said, rocking on his heels. "Your gun. We catch you over the body. She, as I recognize, is one of the circus people and, if I am not mistaken, the wife of the young man who met his demise this morning. You and the lady friend have a little falling-out, Peters?"

A sudden blast of wind plastered my wet pants to my leg, pushed Nelson sideways, and made a groan through the ruins.

"Don't move," came Nelson, fighting the wind.

"I'm not moving unless the wind moves me," I said. Alex, I saw, hadn't been affected by the blast of air. He held the pistol out for Nelson, who examined it with the joy one would expect to see in the eyes of a pearl diver who has just come up with a beauty the size of a marshmallow.

"There are no low-life circus freaks to do battle for you now, Peters," said Nelson. "So Alex and I will just take you back to our little jail, arrange for this body, and have ourselves a chat, a cup of coffee, and a confession or two."

"I didn't kill her," I repeated.

"Oh, yes, you did," he said. Then he looked up into the rain and showed his not too straight and not terrible white teeth. "Good day to spend indoors chatting."

"You . . ."

"What am I, Peters?" he said, losing his joy-of-life attitude. "How the hell do you know what I am? I do more good in this world in one day than you'll do in your whole miserable lifetime. Just ask Alex. Ask him about the parties for the Mex kids I give, the handouts."

"Alex," I said, feeling my back start to sag in pain. "Is he a saint?"

"Let's get back," said Alex, walking past Nelson and heading toward the ridge.

"Tell him, Alex," Nelson shouted. "Tell him."

"Sheriff Nelson is a good man," Alex said, his back still turned. He made it sound like something he was reading on a pack of matches.

"Sheriff," I said, pushing the wet hair from my face and trying to pull my broken-zippered windbreaker close. "There's a dead woman over there. You think we might show her a little respect and let her go in peace without all your elephant crap?"

"Someday," hissed Nelson, "I'm going to be governor of this whole damn state."

"Wouldn't surprise me in the least," I said, following Alex.

chapter 6

Nelson was as good as his word. He put on some clean, dry socks when we got back to the jail and made himself a cup of coffee. Then we sat, him behind his desk with his feet up and a cup of coffee in his hand, Alex standing behind me, and me dripping in a wooden chair across from Nelson.

"Like some coffee?" Nelson asked with a twinkle.

I didn't answer, didn't even let myself sneeze for a second or two, and then let it out.

Nelson scrambled back. "Can't go spreading those germs all around here," he said seriously, shaking the spilled coffee from his hands.

"Maybe we should give him a dry shirt," Alex said behind me.

"All right. All right," Nelson agreed and went back to his feet-up pose. I could hear Alex move behind me, the wooden floor creaking. Behind Nelson's head was a series of framed certificates and plaques. One was from the students of Theodore Roosevelt Elementary School at Mirador for giving a safety lecture back in 1938. Another was for completing an extension course from the University of Southern California in basic civics.

I took the shirt handed to me over my shoulder, removed my jacket and shirt, and put on the dry one, which smelled faintly of alcohol.

"Got a complete sheet on you, Peters," Nelson said, tapping something before him. "Like to know your life story, straight from the Los Angeles PD? I've had it here ever since our last little social encounter."

I said nothing. He sipped and read aloud. "Toby Peters, born Tobias Leo Pevsner. I can see why you might not like the name you were born with, too sort of Jew-sounding. Let's see, now, born Glendale, California, November 14, 1897. Mother died when you were just a baby. Father owned a grocery store. Older brother is an L.A. police lieutenant. You went about a year and a half to junior college and then joined the Glendale police in 1917. Father died in 1932. Your brother was in the first big war, wounded while you stayed back."

"You in the war, Nelson?"

"I was unable to serve," he said. "Let us get back to you. You have been known to consort with known criminals."

"I try to catch them sometimes. It's difficult to catch them unless you get near them. You might ask a real cop sometime."

"Your wife left you," Nelson went on. "You a violent man with women, Peters?"

"I am a pussycat with everyone," I said. "I've been thinking seriously of joining a seminary, Little Brothers of the Meek. I deplore violence, shudder at the sight of blood, and confess to any and all crimes when tight-assed sheriffs frighten me."

Nelson's grimace wouldn't move into a grin. "We shall just see about what frightens you, Peters."

"You know, Nelson, you sound like Richard Loo in a cheap war movie. You'll never get the role. You're too small, too silly-looking, too smug, too transparent, too . . ."

"That's it," shouted Nelson, slamming his coffee cup on the table. "Alex, I think you should take our Mr. Peters here into the back cell and use your powers of persuasion to convince him to confess. I, meanwhile, will see to the body of his unfortunate victim."

Alex didn't reply, so Nelson went on. "You understand, Alex?"

"Sure," said Alex, grabbing my shoulder and pulling me up.

"We will talk a bit later, Mr. Peters, when you have had a few contemplative hours to consider the cleansing nature of confession."

I winked at Nelson, whose teeth gritted together loudly enough to hear. Then he stamped out into the rain. Through the storefront window, Alex and I watched him get into the police car.

"In back," said Alex.

"Hey, it's Nelson you're mad at, not me." I moved ahead of him to the narrow walkway between the two cells. The whole damn jail was no bigger than my Hollywood rented room.

"You'll do," Alex said evenly, pushing me into the second cell, the one furthest from where anyone could hear us.

"I didn't kill that woman, Alex," I said.

He was rolling his sleeves up slowly, apparently not hearing me.

"I'm not going to confess to anything," I said.

"My cousin Lope Obregon," said Alex, facing me. "In the bar."

"Hell, he was drunk and looking for trouble." I backed against the wall, and Alex moved forward. I could feel the vibration of radio music from Hijo's through the thin shared wall.

"Maybe so," agreed Alex. "But he's my cousin."

My minimal sutdy of fear has demonstrated to me that people under its spell are capable of amazing and frightening things. I did what neither Alex nor I expected me to do. Actually, my body did it without my bidding. In fact, given the chance to discuss it with myself, I wouldn't have acted. I threw a hard right, my whole body behind it, in the general direction of Alex's chin. He turned as it came, and I caught him in the Adam's apple. He went backwards, clutching his throat and sucking for air.

"Christ," I shouted. "That's not what I wanted."

Alex was on his knees, taking short breaths, trying not to die. I went for the cell door, slammed it shut behind me, gave it a pull to be sure it was locked, and went for the front of the station.

Alex was still choking behind me, but he was doing something else too, as I discovered a second later when the first bullet pinged off the cell bars behind me. The second bullet hit the big window of the police station. The window cracked and crumbled as I went through the door into the street. I threw my shoulder up to cover my face from the blast of glass.

Two arms grabbed me, and I pulled my fist back madly, determined to get away from Alex now regardless of the cost, because I knew for sure what the cost would be if Alex got his hands on me again.

"Peters," said Elder.

His mustaches were glistening, and his coat was pulled over his shoulders.

"Elder, let's get the hell out of here."

A third shot convinced him, and he turned and leaped into a small gray Ford truck.

"What?"

"Just go, go, go," I said near panic, and he went.

On the way back to the highway, I explained what had happened, and Elder explained that the hour had passed and he had decided to come looking for me in town instead of calling the state police. I told him about Rennata's murder. His head dropped for a particle of a second and came up again.

I told him about the elephant and the drawing made by Rennata, about Nelson's desire to pin the murder on me and my desire to stay alive.

"We'll hide you," he said.

"Bad idea," I said back. "Just have someone pick up my car and drop me off at the highway, along here somewhere."

"You're giving up?"

"If I stay with the circus, you've got some big trouble coming down from the Mirador police," I said.

"And the murders?" said Elder. "You've got a job. Remember, Kelly hired you to find a killer."

"How are you going to hide me in the circus?" I said reasonably.

"If we don't hide you and you don't find the killer," he explained reasonably, "you'll go back to Los Angeles, get picked up, and be back in the Mirador jail. Either that or you'll have to hide in Los Angeles till we find the killer, and we, meaning me, are without experience when it comes to finding killers."

"Right," I said. Night was coming. "I'll need some help. I've got to get some people I trust from L.A. to help me, especially if I've got to do some hiding."

"All right," he agreed. "But you can use me too."

"Elder," I said as evenly as I could, "I can't trust anyone within five miles of this murder including you, Emmett Kelly, or the sheriff of Mirador, especially the sheriff of Mirador."

chapter 7

I made my call to Los Angeles and then put myself in the hands of Elder and Emmett Kelly. What they did with those hands was transform me into a clown. My brother would have said that it didn't take much, but it had to be enough to fool Nelson and Alex, who made it to the circus no more than twenty minutes after us. I had a little blue hat on and a shiny suit with an inflated inner tube inside it. I began to sweat almost immediately and knew that the greasepaint wasn't letting me perspire enough; I was getting sicker by the minute.

Almost any law-enforcement agent, even the dumb cops played by people like Bill Demarest or Nat Pendleton in the movies, would have considered a clown costume.

"I'm going to tear this circus apart, elephant puddle by elephant puddle, until I find Peters," Nelson told Elder through closed teeth. Kelly, I, and four other clowns were within listening distance. I was playing with a fake rope that looked as if I was twirling a lasso, only the lasso was a rigid hoop. It was a third-rate gag but a first-rate disguise.

"Lots of elephants, lots of people," said Elder evenly. He leaned against a huge trunk in Clown Alley, where we were putting on costumes and fixing props. "Besides, Peters isn't here. If he killed Rennata, this is the last place he'd come. He'd get himself torn to pieces."

"Maybe," said Nelson. Alex was looking around at every face, and when he came to mine I concentrated on the little hoop. He fingered his Adam's apple, and his eyes went past me. I was sick of twirling the lasso.

"I don't know where he is," said Elder evenly.

"You are lying," Nelson went on, letting his tongue go over his lower lip.

Elder laughed, a nice deep laugh. "Sheriff, how am I supposed to answer that? Say I'm not lying? Admit that I am, which I am not? Feel free to look around here as much as you want. My guess is that Peters got his car and is back in Los Angeles by now."

Alex wandered over to me slowly, suspiciously. I kept twirling madly. I could feel him behind me, but I didn't look.

"I have taken the precaution of doing just that," sighed Nelson, removing his sweat-stained hat and wiping the band with his dirty handkerchief. I could see Nelson's gray-stubbled chin announcing that he was losing his grip on his minimal appearance and the case.

"Hey," said Alex behind me. Kelly, who was applying the end of his makeup, looked up, hesitated, and went back to finishing his mouth.

"Hey, you," Alex repeated, touching my shoulder.

I turned to him, still twirling, and pointed to myself with my free hand. His eyes were looking into mine.

"How do you do that?" he said, pointing to the twirling rope. I stopped twirling and held out the hoop to him. I could see the black-and-blue mark on his neck, and his voice sounded more than a little raspy. He took the rope and held it up.

"When you are through fooling around like a damn baby," Nelson called to him, "we can get on with catching a killer and, maybe, this time holding onto him."

Alex stiffened at the public dressing-down, and I took the rope from his fingers. Maybe something about the way I took the rope attracted Nelson, who moved two steps toward us away from Elder, cocked his head to one side like a constipated stork, and looked at me.

Kelly stood up and looked at me, but of course he wasn't Kelly as I knew him. He was a sad-faced tramp clown, as sad a face as could be painted on a human. His hands were plunged in his grungy pockets, and he winked at me as Nelson decided to take another step forward.

Before Nelson could challenge me, Kelly reached behind him and picked up a sledgehammer. Nelson hesitated, stopped, and put his hand on his gun. Suspicion had started to turn to more than that.

Kelly put the hammer in my hand and reached into his shaggy pocket to pull out a peanut, which he held up mournfully for us all to see. The other clowns in the tent, six of them, stopped what they were doing and watched. Kelly's tramp went through a weary effort to crush the peanut with his fingers, under his arms, against his head, and by sitting on it. Finally, he dropped it on the ground, reached for the sledgehammer in my hands, and lifted it over his head. Nelson began to draw his gun, and Alex pushed me out of the way to make a plunge at Kelly if he attacked. Kelly brought the hammer down quickly on the peanut on the ground, dropped the hammer, looked down, knelt, and held up the crushed pieces of peanut in his hand.

Behind me I could hear laughter. Alex let out a small chuckle, and Nelson looked relieved. As frightened as I was at the prospect of being carted back for torture in the Mirador jail while wearing a clown suit, even I found Kelly's act funny.

"We are wasting our damn time here," said Nelson in exasperation. "Let's look." Alex followed him out of the tent, with Elder behind them to keep an eye on the Mirador duo.

"Thanks," I said to Kelly.

"Thank Willie," he said. "Willie took over."

"Took over?" I said, trying to sit in a wooden chair in front of the line of mirrors in the tent. I couldn't sit. The costume wouldn't let me.

"When I'm Willie, he takes over. I mean, I always know I'm me, nothing like that, but Willie is a funny man. I'm not funny. I don't even know what makes Willie funny. Most of my act just happened when I made it up while walking around the tent during a show. That bit with the peanut. Willie made it up in England a year ago. People ask me what makes it funny. I don't know. I just do it, and people find it funny. I do another bit with pretending to saw wood. Audiences fall apart. I'm not sure why. Actually, the peanut thing builds up better than that. If you watch the show tonight, you'll see what I mean."

It was nearly time for the show and there wasn't much time to talk, but I asked Kelly a few questions about himself and found out that he was married but not with his wife, that he had two sons, and that he had grown up in Huston, Missouri. He hadn't run away to the circus. He had gone to the big city to get work, the big city being Kansas City, and had tried everything including cleaning milk bottles before getting a job with a company that did advertising films. He created the Willie cartoon. Later, when he was with the circus, he painted circus wagons before he became a performer. For a while, between seasons, he had done a nightclub act with his cartoons. He'd also done a little Broadway, working a few nights in Olsen and Johnson's *Hellzapoppin* and then a comedy called *Keep Off the Grass.*

"Got good reviews for that play," he said. "Met some nice people, Ray Bolger, Jimmy Durante. Nice kid named Jackie Gleason. Durante didn't care for me getting big laughs, though. The circus is harder, but better. Might like to do a movie someday."

"Movie director named Hitchcock has been hanging around the circus today," I said, looking at myself in the mirror and not believing it was me. I tried not to think what would happen if I needed a toilet.

"The circus?"

"Right," I said. "Short, fat, wears neat suits. Looks like he's pouting."

"Oh," said Kelly. "I've seen him. That's Hitchcock the

director? I saw the one with the poisoned milk. Liked it. Something about him I don't like, though."

"The milk wasn't poisoned," I said.

It was now ten minutes before showtime. We could hear the crowd coming in, vendors hawking candy and souvenirs, the lions and tigers catching the scent of the crowd, getting restless and growling into the night. I had an appointment with the one person in the tent this morning I had not talked to. Kelly told me how to get to him, and I walked past the other clowns, into the night and the crowds.

Some adults pretended I wasn't at all unusual. Others nudged their children to look at me. I had a hell of a time making my way with my inner-tube stomach through the crowds shoveling cotton candy into their mouths.

I was just about to enter the sideshow tent which announced the presence of Gargantua when a hand grabbed my arm. I turned, expecting to face Nelson, and found instead a sober man in a faded suit, flannel shirt with no tie, and as sober a face as ever graced American Gothic.

"You a clown?" he asked.

I wondered what the hell else I could be taken for, Eleanor Roosevelt? Instead of answering, I nodded.

"Then do something funny for me and Sis," he said soberly.

Sis was about six years old and came up to my kneecap. She wore a thick, gray-wool sweater a few sizes too big for her, obviously a hand-me-down. Her brown hair was in two braids, and her pale face was turned up at me with more fear than hope of joy. The crowd moved around us. I stuck my thumbs in my ears and wiggled my hands wildly. Sis still looked scared, and Pop was looking down blankly at her. I tried scratching my fake stomach, lifting it up and down, babbling like Bert Lahr. I even considered singing an Eddie Cantor song. It suddenly became very important to me to make this little girl smile. Maybe she was the little girl I would never have. I could imagine her next week on her farm with the unsmiling but probably loving Pop. I could imagine her looking out over the fields of whatever the hell Pop grew and petting her dog. Damn the circus.

I grabbed the man's hand and guided it out in front of him. Then I pretended I was seeing the hand for the first time. I put one foot up on it as if to rest it, and then, ignoring truth and gravity, I raised my other foot as if to rest it also on his arm. Obviously, I fell on my rear in the dirt. I bounced on my inner tube and felt the pain in my back. Without the tube, I would have been bound for the hospital. With it, I felt like hell. I had seen Buster Keaton do the same gag onstage. I never knew how he could do it. I still didn't.

Sis wasn't laughing, but there was definitely a smile on her face when I looked up at her. Something touched the corners of Pop's mouth too, but there wasn't enough there to call it a smile. Some people in the crowd who had watched my act laughed. I picked myself up awkwardly and had a sense of why people wanted to be clowns. They had laughed at me when I wanted them to. Usually, people laugh at me when I don't want them to. It was almost as good as being a private detective and just as bad on the back.

I was on my knees when Pop and Sis walked away to look for a new adventure. I got up and limped into the tent. A few people were blocking the front of a big cage, but the crowd wasn't large. It was almost time for the circus to begin.

I looked around for Henry, the keeper, and saw him sitting on an upside-down bucket, apparently counting the bristles on a broom. I walked over to him as a few more people left the tent. I was aware of animals pacing in cages all around me and the acrid smell of creatures with bulk, fur, and toilet habits that weren't those of humans.

"You Henry?" I said, standing over him.

He looked up, a lanky creature with an open, unlined face and straw hair that fell in strands over his forehead. "Henry," he acknowledged.

"I'm . . ."

"The police guy," he finished. The clown costume had fooled Henry for not even an instant.

"Right," I said. "Elder told you I have some questions."

He nodded without speaking and went on looking for something among the bristles of the broom.

"What do you know about this morning?" I asked quietly, as a few more stragglers went out of the tent heading for the big top.

"Monkeys," he said. "I know monkeys. Big ones mostly. I'm intense with monkeys."

"Intense?"

"Mr. Ringling said I was once," he explained.

"No," I said, trying to readjust the hat on my head. It was small and cardboard, which didn't bother me, but the rubber band holding it was cutting into my chin. "Tanucci and his wife, the younger Tanuccis, are dead, murdered," I said. "Did you see anyone fooling with the harness and rigging this morning?"

"I am poor with cats, horses, and people," answered Henry, examining one strand of straw that caught his eye. "Not intense with them. Just ain't."

"Few of us are," I tried. "You didn't see anything?"

Henry stopped looking at the broom and closed his eyes to think. I had the impression that he had learned to do this to convince others that he was doing what he really could not do, think. I watched politely while his eyes went tighter and tighter and then relaxed.

"Nope," he said, getting up and holding the broom out ahead of him. I followed him toward the cage where the small crowd had gathered and could see that one person remained in front of it. His back was turned, but I recognized the form.

"Mr. Hitchcock," I said. He turned and saw me, and so did the mass of darkness in the cage. His bellow shook me and probably the walls of the tent. Gargantua began to rattle the bars of his cage. He reached down, grabbed his tire, and began banging against the bars of his cage as he bared his teeth at me, and large yellow teeth they were.

"I think," said Hitchcock evenly, "that he doesn't like you."

"An understatement," I said, worrying about the bars of the cage.

"Chrome steel," said Henry without emotion. "He can't get out."

"That's what Carl Denham said about King Kong, and look what he did to New York," I answered.

Henry gave Gargantua the broom. The gorilla took it, was about to throw it, and then became curious.

"Don't like clowns," said Henry. "Sometimes he don't care much. Some clowns."

The other animals were reacting to Gargantua, starting to growl and complain. I went for the tent flap with Hitchcock waddling beside me.

"Mr. Peters," he panted. "You are Mr. Peters?"

"Right," I said, stepping outside and trying to rub my back under the inner tube. Most of the crowd was in the big top now, and the band started up with a familiar circus song whose name I didn't know.

"Why, may I inquire, are you wearing a costume?" he said with dignity.

"Simple. The police are after me for murder, murder I didn't commit. They are also unhappy about my poking a policeman and running away. I'm trying to catch the real murderer and save my life."

"That," sighed Hitchcock, "is quite interesting."

"There's a difference between interesting and fun," I said, looking around for Alex or Nelson.

"Not as far as I'm concerned," he said.

"You haven't remembered anything about this morning, have you?" I took a few steps away from the tent. The cats had brought their noise level down to a growl.

"Nothing whatsoever," he said.

"I thought you were going back to Los Angeles today," I said.

"I am," he said. "Just as soon as I see tonight's performance. A murder," he went on, savoring the word and then backing away from it when he repeated it, "a murder."

Maybe I would have thought of another question, maybe an important one that would have cracked the case, but I spotted Alex coming around a tent about forty feet away. He might wonder why a clown wasn't with the other clowns. I lifted my hat to Hitchcock and went toward the big top as quickly as my costume and back would let me. I could feel the wet mud oozing under my shoes. I was afraid my costume might come apart. It reminded me of the time I was in kindergarten back in 1904 or 1905. I was spending a few months with my aunt in Chicago. It was Halloween. I wore a paper devil's costume she had made for me. It started to come apart on the way to school, and I was scared through the whole morning that it would all come off and I'd be in school in my underwear. Each movement had terrified me. Ever since then, I've hated the idea of wearing a costume. The clown suit was no exception. I was afraid Alex would chase me right into the light inside the tent I was heading for and into the middle of the ring, where I'd trip and my costume would come off.

I didn't know if Alex was after me, but I kept moving toward the music, the light, the big tent as if I were late for my act. I went through a small flap and found myself right next to the band. A tuba blasted in my ear. I looked down and saw that the round piece of metal on top of the drum an old guy in a maroon uniform was playing was rotting with age or accident and had been placed behind the tuba player and out of sight of the crowd. That was the way the whole circus operated, on the surface, a thin, fragile surface.

I began twirling my lasso furiously and headed away from the tent flap and the band. Some wire acts were just coming down. One of them had been using a bear; and the bear, the same one I had run into earlier, went by and took a swipe at me. I jumped back, and the crowd near us roared with laughter.

The band stopped and the tent went dim. I looked out into the arena and saw nothing. The ringmaster announced nothing, and then I saw Willie walk out, Emmett Kelly's Willie.

The audience sounds were loud, but they went down as he moved forward and began to plant imaginary seeds in a victory garden in the center ring. As he planted, he also ate some of the seeds. Soon there were no seeds. He took off his hat to scratch his head, and there was a frog perched there. He spent a few minutes trying without success to determine where the frog sound was coming from. The crowd roared.

Then he picked up a broom and began to sweep or pretend to sweep. It took me and Willie a few seconds to see that he could also sweep the spotlight that lit him up. The spotlight grew a bit smaller as he swept it, and then it tried to run away. Willie chased it, holding onto his hat with one hand and the broom with the other. Gradually the circle of light got tired and Willie began to sweep it smaller and smaller until there was only a yellow spot about the size of a plate. He reached under his jacket, pulled out a dustpan, put it down, swept the last circle of light into the pan, and the tent went dark.

There was a beat of silence and then thunderous applause in the darkness. I was crying. I didn't know what the hell I was crying about, and I didn't want that light to come on and people to see me, but it came on. Two boys, fat kids stuffing their faces with popcorn, looked at me. One pointed and spit out about half a pound and laughed. I walked away and out the same tent flap I had come in, expecting to run into the waiting arms of Alex the angry cop, but I didn't. Alex wasn't there. Hitchcock wasn't there. The band struck up behind me, and I walked slowly away, determined that if there was a threat to Emmett Kelly, it had to be stopped.

I stayed in the shadows, moved past tents and wagons, people talking in concession stands, and to a wagon I had been told to find marked with a big red number forty-five. Elder and I had agreed to stay away from Kelly's wagon, the clown tent, and Elder's office wagon, in case Nelson decided to look where he had already seen me or might look.

I knocked at the door of forty-five, and it opened. Peg was startled for a second and then put out her hand to help me up.

I had trouble getting through the door with my inner tube and ache, but we popped me in.

"Nice place," I said, starting to take off my pants.

She was wearing a robe and pajamas. Her hair was down, and she looked comfortable and comforting.

"Hold it," she said.

"Don't get me wrong," I said, continuing. "I've got to get out of this tube and sit down. My back hurts, and I miss the feeling of just getting off my legs. I'm not going to attack you in a clown suit."

"Or any other way?" she asked with a smile, watching me struggle.

"Depends on if you keep laughing at me like that or give me a hand."

She gave me a hand, getting close enough for me to decide that she smelled good, not perfume good but clean good. As soon as I had inched out of the tube after removing my pants, I sat in a chair in my shorts, still wearing my clown makeup, tore off the hat, rubbed the indentation under my chin from the rubber band, and scratched my stomach furiously.

Peg was holding her stomach with laughter.

"I'd rather face Alex in that Mirador cell than put that costume back on," I said. "You've got a great laugh."

"Thanks," she said. "Want some coffee?"

"Thanks." I got up and found a towel in a corner near a mirror. "Can I use this?"

She told me to go ahead, and I removed the makeup. It took me awhile to find me, and I didn't get it all off, but it was enough off me for me to be comfortable. I looked around the small room. Peg had done what she could to make it look like home. Curtains, a quilt on the cot, photographs on the wall of a family that was probably hers, a small table with a cloth, three chairs, a small icebox under the window.

"Nice," I said, going back to the table.

"It's enough," she said, handing me a cup of coffee with

one hand and a doughnut with the other. I was hungry and stuffed the doughnut in my mouth.

"You wouldn't have another two or three doughnuts?" I asked with my mouth full. She grinned and reached back through a cloth covering a cabinet to pull out a plate with two more doughnuts.

"The start of real romance," I said, gulping down some coffee.

"You look silly," she said.

"Try to ignore it," I suggested, choking on the last bite of my second doughnut.

"Can't," she said.

"You really look great," I said.

"You don't," she answered.

"I give up," I said, and I did, for the moment. "Will you marry me?"

"You serious?" she said.

"Hell, no," I said, going for the last of the coffee and handing the cup to her in hope of a refill. "Don't you know what you're supposed to say?"

She got up, pulled her robe around her, turned her back, and poured more coffee.

"Nope," she said. "I don't know much about man-and-woman games."

"Sorry," I said.

"Don't be." She turned and handed me the cup, looking into my eyes with a soft smile. "I don't go to movies much, just circuses."

"I'd like to take you to a movie," I said, accepting the cup and deciding to try to do some dunking with the final doughnut. "You make a mean doughnut."

"Stole it from the mess truck."

"You know how to steal a good doughnut."

We sat watching me try not to lose any of the soggy doughnut until the whole thing was gone. I sat back, wishing I had my pants on and something over my chest besides the purple silk clown's shirt. Peg was looking at me with a soft amusement that might turn to more, and I was trying to think of something to say that wouldn't be a game when the knock came.

"Who is it?" she asked, with just enough touch of fear to show she cared.

"Elder," came the voice.

She told him to come in, and he did. At the top of the step, he looked at both of us, me with my pants off, Peg in her pajamas and robe. Something like anger crossed his face and then disappeared.

"Some visitors from Los Angeles," he said, pointing to the door, through which came the bizarre trio that passes in this life as my best and only friends.

"Shelly, Jeremy, Gunther. Close the door."

And they did.

chapter 8

"You look like a grape popsicle," Sheldon Minck observed through his thick glasses. Shelly is about five five, fat, fifty-five, bald, smokes very wet cigars, and has dirty fingers and questionable habits which make for particular problems since he is a dentist, the dentist with whom I share an office. More accurately, he sublets a closet to me on the fourth floor of the Farraday Building, the last refuge of forgotten dentists, detectives, pornographers, and agents without clients in various fields of life.

"I've had a difficult day, Shel," I said. "I'll explain."

My other two guests nodded in understanding. They are as much in contrast as two humans could be unless we also made one a woman and turned one black or brown or tan. As it is, Jeremy Butler stands about six three and weighs in at just short of 250 pounds, which is rather awesome for a poet and the owner-manager of the Farraday Building. Jeremy had once been a professional wrestler. He now wrestles with meters and the grime that threatens to take over his property. In contrast to Jeremy is Gunther Wherthman, who stands no more than four feet high and is certainly a very little person, a midget, who speaks with a precise Swiss accent and wears precise clean suits with vests. His fingernails are never dirty, and he makes a living by translating books and articles from German, French, Italian, Spanish, Polish, and Danish into English. Gunther got me the room in Mrs. Plaut's boardinghouse in Hollywood after the place I lived in got crushed by a wrecker.

The first piece of business was to clear the room by asking Elder and Peg to give us some time together. Peg went behind a towel hung in a corner and changed, while the four of us said nothing.

Peg smiled at me on the way out, and as soon as the door closed, Gunther, seated on the bed so his feet would touch the floor, said, "You suspect her of something?"

"No," I told him. "Just want to be sure."

Gunther nodded in agreement. He wore a beautiful little chesterfield coat.

Jeremy Butler pulled out one of the chairs at the table with a lobster hand and sat carefully. The chair didn't break. He unbuttoned his flannel jacket and looked at me.

"Been brushing your teeth?" asked Shelly.

"Shel, what are you doing here? I called Jeremy and Gunther."

"I ran into Jeremy, and he told me you needed help," said Shelly, removing his cigar to examine the end. His glasses slipped down his nose, and he almost poked himself in the eye with the cigar stub to keep them from dropping. "Besides, they needed a car."

Shelly's 1937 Ford was as filthy as his 1914 office, but it ran and defied reason by never causing him trouble in spite of his neglect.

"I'm sorry, Toby," Jeremy began.

"OK," I said with my hand up. "Shelly can help. We've got a murder or two here, animals, people, and maybe more to come. The local police think I did it, and if they get their hands on me, I will probably lose my hands. So we've got to find the killer and protect the circus, and we've got to do it fast before there are no more performers to protect. Oh, yes, we've also got a runaway elephant."

"Proceed," said Gunther calmly, and I proceeded. I told them the whole story. Jeremy and Gunther sat quietly, listening. Shelly was soon floating somewhere, thinking of cavities.

"So," said Gunther, "it seems an easy process. We list everyone who stood in the tent when the unfortunate Mr. Tanucci died. We then make that list smaller if we can."

"The killer already has made it smaller," Shelly said with a satisfied grin.

"How did you get Mildred to let you go?"

"I told her you needed my help."

"Mildred would gladly see me turned over to the Japanese," I told him.

"You wrong my Mildred," countered Shelly.

"Toby," said Gunther softly. "May I continue?"

I apologized, and he continued. "We may, for the moment, assume that the Tanuccis are not responsible for the murder of their own clan. This may turn out to be a false assumption, but given our group size . . ."

"Reasonable," agreed Jeremy.

"We eliminate Toby," Gunther went on. "May we eliminate the doctor? He is quite old, yes?"

"Probably," I said. "It would take a quick hand to cut that harness and someone with a steady hand to gun down Rennata so neatly on the beach."

"Good," continued Gunther. "We then have Mr. Elder, who you were talking to, which eliminates him. . . ."

"From stealing the harness," Jeremy said quickly. "He might have an accomplice."

My chest thumped. Peg might be such an accomplice. "Maybe," I agreed.

"Now, we eliminate you," added Gunther, "and may I assume we eliminate Alfred Hitchcock?"

"No," shouted Shelly, leaping to his feet and pointing his cigar at me. "Movie directors can be killers."

"Shelly," I said in exasperation, "why would Alfred Hitchcock be killing people and elephants in the circus?"

"Material for movies," he said triumphantly. He began to pace the small floor while presenting his theory. "Movie director goes crazy. Can't think of stories for his movies. Maybe he was scared by a clown or a wombat when he was a kid."

"What the hell is a wombat?" I said.

"Marsupial," explained Gunther, "large, rodent appearance. Native, I believe, to Tasmania."

"What the hell has a wombat got to do with this case?" I said.

"Hitchcock may have . . ."

"Hitchcock, hell. Shel, just stand still and let Gunther finish."

Shelly went back to his chair, folded his arms, and pouted while Gunther continued. "Therefore, our most likely suspects; are Henry, the animal keeper; Agnes Sudds, the serpent lady, and Thomas Paul, the curious double-faced man for whom you have no affection."

It sounded reasonable to me.

"Therefore, if we also eliminate Emmett Kelly," continued Gunther, "it would be best to use our resources in watching the three prime suspects rather than trying to anticipate potential victims."

It sounded perfectly good to me, which made me wonder for a few seconds why I hadn't thought of it, but only for a few seconds. I hadn't thought of it for just that reason—it was reasonable. I was not used to operating from reason.

"It has problems," said Jeremy Butler, "but it seems the most reasonable to me too."

"I'm sorry to bring you down here," I said. "Thanks for the help."

"I welcome the chance to see the circus," said Jeremy, standing and examining Peg's posters. "I'll get a sense of it, perhaps already have, for my life poem. The elephants' ears like huge leaves. The burning smell of animal life."

"That's donkey piss," explained Shelly.

"Thanks, Shel."

Shelly looked satisfied.

I got up slowly. A debate then began over how to treat my once again sore back. Shelly had his pain pills and Jeremy his experience. The back wasn't bad enough for both yet, so I went with Jeremy's treatment. I got on my stomach and let him work with his powerful grip. A second of pain and then the relief, not perfect but much better.

I deployed the troops by assigning Shelly to Henry Brainfeeble Yew, assuming Henry was the only one Shelly could watch without being spotted unless Henry was putting on an act. Gunther I sent to Agnes Sudds and the slithering Abdul, and Jeremy to Thomas Paul, should the creature show up as he had promised. I would stay with Peg and try to keep an eye on Elder. It seemed reasonable. We called Elder in to help us find our suspects.

"Don't I know you?" Elder said to Gunther as I explained our plan, at least all of it except the part about my watching him.

"Yes," said Gunther with dignity and an accent. "I worked briefly in the circus when I came to this country. Our paths crossed. While I respect it, it is not the life with which I wish to be identified. Please do not take offense."

Elder touched his mustache and nodded politely.

I wondered how painful the experience of coming back to the circus would be for Gunther. I hadn't thought about it when I sent for him. I had sent for a friend and forgotten that he was a sensitive small human who was trying desperately to achieve some dignity and distance from the public view of midgets as curiosities and freaks. I didn't think he could do it with people on the street. It takes knowing someone not to see him.

Elder led everyone out after we agreed to meet again at midnight or when we were sure the people we were watching were well tucked in for the night. It was the best we could do for the moment.

Peg came back with a pair of pants for me, a shirt, and my zipperless jacket.

"Coast is clear," she said. "The sheriff has gone. I think he's convinced you went back to Los Angeles."

I started to dress, put one foot in my pants and tore some stitches. Peg sat down and watched me. The band struck a loud chord far off, and the crowd went, "Ahhhh."

"Martin the Great," she said. "Sways on a flexible bar fifty feet high. They think he's going to fall. A good trick."

"Dangerous?" I asked, buttoning my shirt.

"You're one button off," she said. "Not too dangerous. Emmett Kelly told me once the most dangerous act he ever saw was a guy named Fitzgerald at a small circus back in Missouri. Fitzgerald worked a high wire without a net, dangerous stuff, didn't give a darn for the audience. Didn't make easy things look hard. Tried to make everything look easy. Wouldn't play for a bow, just walked off when his act was finished. Kelly says he was the greatest, but no one but the circus people ever knew it."

"What happened to Fitzgerald?" I asked, getting the buttons right.

"Fell," she said with a sad shrug. "Kelly says almost no one even noticed when he went down. They were all looking at a third-rate family act in center ring."

"Tough," I said, dressed and looking at her.

"Circus," she said. "What now?"

"As they say on the radio, we wait."

We talked for a while about my father, my brother, the war, the price of gas, her father, her mother, Elder, and snow. I don't remember how we got to snow. I do remember how I moved over and sat next to her on the bed, and she didn't complain. My arm went up to her shoulder while she talked about what she liked about the circus. I don't think anything much would have happened even if Emmett Kelly hadn't knocked at the wagon door. I don't know. I'll never know, but knock he did.

"Come in," she called, looking in my eyes.

"Some grippers spotted Greta," he said, still in his Willie costume.

"Greta?"

"The elephant Rennata took with her, the one on the beach," he explained.

Peg got up. "Where is she?"

"Trucking her back," he said, trying to catch his breath. "Someone shot her, but she'll probably be all right, according to Doc Ogle. It takes a big bullet and a good shot to bring down a bull."

"That's one saved," I sighed.

"Yeah," agreed Kelly, "but we've got a bigger problem. Now a lion is loose."

I followed Kelly into the night with Peg behind us. I could see circus people running madly and as quietly as they could with chairs and sticks in their hands, poking into corners, into tents, behind wagons, dark figures. The band in the big top seemed to be playing a march just for them. Musical chairs. Maybe "The Stars and Stripes Forever" would stop, and so would they. It stopped, but they didn't.

Peg was shivering beside me. The night was cold, but that wasn't why she was shivering. "They don't know in the top, do they?"

"No," said Kelly. "I've seen a panic. We've got to try to find the cat before the show ends."

Kelly, looking even more worried than in the center ring, hurried off to look for the lion with no weapon other than his prop broom. I didn't even have my petrified lasso, and my gun had been confiscated by the Mirador police.

"So," I said to Peg, taking her hand, "we look for a runaway lion. But first we find out what happened."

We hurried back to Henry's tent, but Henry wasn't there. Gargantua was there, but he didn't seem to recognize me. He just sat on the floor of his cage eating something that could have been a cabbage, a radio, or a human head. Some people were standing near a cage in the rear. A lion was in the cage.

"You found him," I shouted to Elder, running forward. The blond, tan man at his side was dressed in white tights and jacket. From a distance he looked twenty. Up close he looked fifty. I recognized him.

"No," said Elder. "Sandoval came in to check on the cats and saw the cage open. Only one cat had gotten out. The other one stayed."

"Someone opened up the cage," Sandoval said with a broad gesture. "Why would someone do such a thing? I need that cat for my act. He can do a rollover . . ."

"Is he dangerous?" I asked, gripping Peg's hand.

"Of course," said Sandoval with indignation. "What is the point of working with cats that are not dangerous? I am an artist, not a sideshow trick."

"Sorry," I said.

"Sandoval," said Elder, putting his hand on the performer's shoulder and looking into his eyes. "You've got to keep your act going tonight till I tell you to stop. Do it twice if you have to. We've got to have time to catch the cat."

"Without the rollover?" Sandoval complained.

"I'm afraid so," said Elder seriously.

Sandoval shrugged and gave a show-must-go-on smile, turned, and hurried out of the tent.

"Chances are the cat will stay nearby," said Elder, looking at me and Peg. "Well, let's look. His name is Puddles, but he doesn't answer to any name. If you find him, let out a yell and get something between you and him."

"No accident, was it?" I asked.

"You kidding?" said Elder. "Whoever did it pried the damn lock off. Now, let's find Puddles."

chapter 9

I found puddles a few feet away, but finding Puddles was another story. Actually, it's this story.

"Why do they call the lion Puddles?" I asked, moving into a nearby tent. "I thought lions were called things like Rajah or King."

Peg followed me into the tent. There was a single light overhead, a not-many-watts yellow bulb. It looked like a dressing tent.

"Some animal trainers give their lions and tigers names to be respected," Peg explained. "Maybe just to remember to respect them. Others give them nicknames like Puddles to make them seem less frightening."

Something moved in a corner behind an open trunk. I pushed Peg and tripped. "Out," I yelled.

"Nothing here," came a voice from behind the trunk, and Agnes Sudds emerged with a red spangled cap on her orange head.

I got up, prepared to keep my distance from her and determined not to ask about Abdul.

"If I find him," she said, looking back, "Abdul will hold

him till help comes. Don't worry about me."

Since I hadn't been worrying about Agnes, I didn't say anything. I wondered if Gunther was hovering somewhere nearby, watching her.

When Agnes was gone, I called, "Gunther" softly.

"His name is Puddles," said Peg when Gunther appeared, and I explained quickly about the plan to tail the prime suspects. Peg said nothing. It wasn't bright enough to see her eyes clearly, but something troubled her. Maybe she wondered if someone, me, was trailing her.

"Now, wait . . ." I began but didn't get far because someone ran into the tent, panting. It was Shelly. He went to a nearby coil of rope and sat down with one hand over the approximate area of his heart.

"Lost . . . him," he wheezed. "Saw . . . you . . . come . . . in . . . here . . . and . . ."

The distinct nearby roar of a very large animal stopped Shelly, who looked around the tent in fear. Sweat had dropped his eyebrows. "What?" he asked, trying to stand. The coil was too low. He sat back down again.

"Quiet," I said. "It's Puddles."

"Puddles?"

"The lion," Peg whispered, looking into the darkness.

"I don't see his cage," Shelly whispered, getting the idea.

"He escaped," said Peg. "Someone let him out."

Shelly stood up with several "damns." The next proud roar was louder than the last one and definitely in the tent. Agnes and Abdul had either done a rotten job of lion searching or had let us walk into a pride of lions.

Shelly's glasses had slipped to the tip of his nose, and he didn't see the wooden chair near the door. He tumbled over it and let out a yell of fear.

"My faithful retainer," I said. Nobody laughed, not even Puddles, who came bounding out from behind a stack of boxes to see what we were making so much noise about. Puddles was big. His teeth were big, his orange-black mane was big, and he was standing about ten feet in front of me. I reached behind me while I looked at him in the dim light and tried to grasp the chair. It wasn't there, and Puddles took a step toward us.

"The chair," I said very quietly. Someone, certainly not Shelly, who I could hear going, "Uh . . . uh . . . uh . . ." at the entrance, handed me the chair.

"She's afraid," said Peg. "Look at her eyes."

Puddles' eyes were yellow with black hatred in their centers, and they were getting bigger and bigger. I put the chair between me and Puddles.

"I'll try not to frighten her," I said with what I hoped was bitter sarcasm. It probably came out more like hysterical fear.

Puddles swiped at the chair with a paw and let out a growl. I held onto the chair.

"That's part of her act," Peg whispered.

"What's the next part?"

"You put the chair down and stick your head in her mouth," Peg explained behind me while Shelly switched to, "Oh no . . . oh no . . . oh no."

"I think I'll improvise instead," I said, bringing the chair in front of me. Puddles cocked her head and looked puzzled. This was not the act, and I was not the trainer. She had latched onto something familiar in unfamiliar territory, but I wasn't playing the game.

"I am not putting this chair down and sticking my head in her mouth," I said through my teeth.

"Toby, do it, for God's sake," whimpered Shelly.

For a wild fraction of a second, I lost all fear. Once a woman in Pamona, or it may have been Palm Springs, told me she had jumped from a roof without planning to do it, just because she found herself looking down and suddenly lost touch of what it would mean. One thing that saved me from the jaws of Puddles was Puddles' mouth. It was open and full of saliva and teeth.

"I'm not putting my head in that mouth," I cried.

"I put my hands in worse mouths than that every day," Shelly pleaded.

"Forget it, Shel or do it yourself."

Puddles took a tentative swipe again, but it didn't have the showmanship of the first swing. It didn't even have a roar.

"She's making up her mind, I think," said Peg.

"I'm going to hit the sonofabitch in the head with the chair. When I do it, run like hell," I said, trying to smile reassuringly at the lion who looked into my face. I was probably uglier than the lion, but she seemed curious.

"That's a stinking plan," shrieked Shelly.

"I have none better," I said, raising the chair slowly. "Get ready, Peg."

"Toby," she said, clutching my arm. "You could hurt her."

"I hope so," I said. "I really hope so."

Puddles seemed to understand something of what was going on. She opened her mouth, bared her teeth, roared and eliminated the last of the space between us. The chair should have come down in her face, but I knew it was still up in the air, maybe floating up there with my hands and arms attached. A marvel of the universe.

"Stop that," came a voice from behind me as Puddles was about to eat my cheek. When the voice hit, Puddles took one step backward, hesitated, and looked as if she were going to spring.

"I said stop," shouted the blond lion tamer Sandoval, stepping to my side. The lion backed up two steps and growled.

"Chair," he said in a confident voice. "Hand me the chair quickly."

I pleaded with my arms to respond, and they did. I thanked them and watched the trainer step forward, driving Puddles back.

"Now," he said commandingly, "we go back to your cage. Right *now*. I will like you very much if you go back to your cage, but I will not like you very much if you do not."

I don't know if the lion understood the words spoken with

a European accent I couldn't pinpoint, but she knew she was in the presence of the boss.

"Now lie down," the man commanded softly. "Down." And the lion went down.

"Thanks," I said, without looking back at Peg, who clutched my arm, or Shelly, who was breathing loudly enough to rouse the Japanese at sea.

"Very slowly," he said. "Very slowly go back to the tent where the cage is, and bring Henry and some help. Bring the roll cage in the corner. Quick, but slow."

I moved with what I thought was a quick but slow pace back through the tent flap, pulling Peg with me. Shelly sat petrified in the dirt, his eyes fixed on Puddles.

"Let's go, Shel," I said, reaching down for him, but he didn't move and I didn't have time to wait. Outside the tent, Peg let go of my arm and I ran for the tent a few dozen yards away. Gargantua was dozing. So was Henry.

"Hurry," I shouted. "The pull cage. Lion's in the tent over there." I pointed meaninglessly.

Henry moved faster than I thought a Henry could move behind the lion cage and pulled a smaller cage on wheels that didn't look big enough to hold Puddles.

"Gimme a hand," grunted Henry. "I ain't endowed enough."

With my endowment and his we got the small cage rolling and out into the night. I glanced in the direction of the big top and could see a few people leaving. The music was going furiously, but whatever the stall, it wasn't working for some of the people.

"I seen the guy who done it," Henry said. "Skunking around. Little fat guy, sweaty guy with no hair and glasses."

"Not him," I panted. Shelly had managed to get spotted by Henry within five minutes of following him. We went through the flap of the storage tent. Nothing had changed. Neither man nor animal had moved.

The sudden arrival of Henry and me startled Puddles, who stood up.

"Shhh," said Sandoval, putting his finger to his lips. "You back there, be quiet. Be quiet."

"That's him," shouted Henry, pointing at Shelly.

"Forget him," I said to Henry. "Open the cage."

Unsure of whether to watch Shelly or Puddles, Henry opened the door of the cage and said, "Open."

The tamer coaxed the lion toward him with his hand. "Come, yes, come with me," he said, showing teeth which gleamed even in this dim light. The music of "The Washington and Lee March" filtered in from the big top and seemed to give Puddles the feeling that this was something a bit more familiar.

"Yes," said the tamer, crouching and backing up next to the cage. "You didn't want to run away, did you? No. You just ran to the closest dark place. Now, into the cage. Go, Go."

And into the cage went Puddles with only one brief pause to swipe a paw at the tamer and try to rip his right arm to the bone from elbow to wrist.

"Ahhh," gargled Shelly, as the tamer pushed the door closed on the big cat.

"Wheel her back," he said to Henry, hardly noticing that he might be bleeding to death.

"Can't do it by myself," bleated Henry, showing no great interest in the maimed man before him.

"Shelly, get off your behind and help," I shouted, walking over to Sandoval, who showed nothing, didn't even touch his arm.

Shelly managed to get up and over to Henry, who eyed him with great suspicion.

"Get the doctor," I said.

"No," said the tamer in the same commanding tone he had used with Puddles. "First get that cat out of here."

Shelly and Henry obeyed as quickly as they could and made a not very fast exit, pulling the rattling caged lion outside.

"The cat could not see me reacting," explained the tamer when the animal was gone. "If she saw me showing fear, I'd never be able to use her again."

"You may never use that arm again," I said, looking for

something to slow down the bleeding. I took off my jacket and wrapped it around his arm. He sagged back, and I put out both arms to catch him. He felt cold.

The blood soaked my jacket red almost instantly. I let one hand reach for the chair, set it right, and guided the tamer into it. He nodded thanks as people rushed into the tent around us.

"Doc's on the way," said someone.

Sandoval didn't even nod. Elder was there, propping him up, and so were two or three others I hadn't met. Then Doc Ogle came in with his plaid bag. He squinted, trying to find his patient.

"Here, Doc," said Elder.

The doctor came over to us and looked down at me with obvious disdain.

"Not me," I said. "Him. His arm."

Then the doctor spotted what everyone in the tent had seen the second they came in.

"If you hide the man," he said irritably, "how the hell am I supposed to treat him? What happened to him?"

"Lion," I said.

The small crowd backed away, and Peg came through to stand at my side.

"Who put this filthy jacket on this wound?" said the doctor, moving his head inches from the arm as he flung my jacket in the corner. "Man gets bit by a damn lion and you push the germs in."

"I'm sorry," I said.

"Stop the bleeding and kill the patient," said the doctor to himself, pressing the wound with his hands. The tamer grimaced but didn't let out a sound. The bleeding slowed. "Pressure," said the old doctor.

"It wasn't a bite," I said. "The lion tore his arm with his nails."

"Claws," corrected the doctor. "Well, pick him up and we'll get him to my wagon. He'll be all right. I'll be sewing on that arm for two hours, but he'll be all right. Now, if we can just declare a cease-fire for an hour or two . . ."

He had no ending for his observation. Two men started to help Sandoval out. His yellow mane was sagging.

"Thanks," I whispered to him. He had probably saved me from his own fate or worse, but he didn't hear me.

Shelly came running in just as the crowd left. "This is not good for me," he said seriously. "It really isn't. I'm not used to this stuff with animals. Did you see the tricuspid on that baby?"

I had been chased by an elephant and almost killed by a lion in one day. The closest I had been to an animal outside of the Griffith Park Zoo was a police horse, and I didn't much like it.

"Let's go back to my wagon," said Peg to me quietly. I liked the invitation.

"Good idea," agreed Shelly, picking up the words. "I could use a cup of coffee."

We walked back to Peg's wagon through the crowd streaming out of the big top. Some faces were tired, some flushed with recent memory, none aware that they had almost had a lion in their laps.

The three of us had coffee, and Shelly kept talking. It was clear that he wasn't going to leave until someone told him where he was sleeping. There was no point in sending him to watch Henry. He had already been spotted. So he talked of past patients, bicuspid articles he would never write, and the state of restoration of his favorite customer's mouth. Mr. Stange had but one crusty tooth, a small scenic reproduction of one representative of Monument Valley. On this decaying piece of enamel, Shelly planned to reconstruct a mouth full of false teeth plus some experimental creations which were to be the envy of the county dental association. I felt some pity for Mr. Stange, in spite of the fact that he had once tried to hold Shelly up and had wrecked our office in the process. As I was about to leap on Shelly and kill him, a knock came at the door. Peg looked at me in apology and shrugged.

"Come in."

And in came Gunther and Jeremy.

Gunther sat on the bed next to Shelly, whose mind was back in our office in Mr. Stange's mouth. Gunther looked decidedly dejected.

"I lost her," he said. "I found her and then I lost her."

"So," I said to Peg. "Agnes, who was found inside the tent with Puddles, could have let him out."

"But," said Jeremy, putting his massive bulk into the chair near me, "Thomas Paul could not have. He was in the big tent all through the show. I found him quickly and watched him. When the show ended, I asked a father and son sitting next to him if Paul had been there all through the show. Paul's face is not forgettable. He was sitting there when the father and son came in half an hour before the show started. I'm sure he didn't know I was watching him. Strange man. He was more interested in the show than anyone I have ever seen at a wrestling match. I cannot always fathom the human mind."

"So," I said, "that lets Mr. Paul out."

"Perhaps not," said Gunther. His hand went to his neck as if to loosen his tie, but his sense of decorum got the better of his instinct and the hand came down. "Perhaps it is Mr. Paul who has an accomplice."

"Agnes," shouted Shelly.

"Possible," I said, pouring the last of Peg's coffee for the group. "But why the hell would Paul want to ruin the circus?"

No one knew. Peg smiled at me, and I suggested that we all go out and find someplace for my troupe to sleep.

"Perhaps we should stay near our charges, our assignments," said Gunther.

I convinced them to call it a night and went outside with them, whispering to Peg that I would be back soon. People in costume were milling about, still up from their performance, talking about how it went, the murders, the runaway animals. We found Emmett Kelly in his wagon, and I asked him if he could put my friends up.

"We'll find room," said Kelly soberly.

"I'll find somewhere else to sleep," I said sacrificially.

"No need for that," said Kelly. "We'll make room."

Then Kelly looked at me and understood.

"I'm sorry about the lion," Shelly said.

"It's OK, Shel," I grinned.

"I didn't want to hurt him," he said, taking Emmett Kelly's bed when Kelly moved to search for some bedding for the others. "I just wanted to frighten him a little."

"Sure, Shel," I said, backing out of the door with no desire to hear the tale the pudgy dentist would spend part of the night telling. I said good night to Kelly, Gunther, and Jeremy. Jeremy was already comfortably on the floor. Poor Gunther was looking for a place to change into the pajamas and robe he would magically produce from somewhere.

"One good thing," said Kelly to me as I started to close the door. "They found the missing elephant."

"Now all we need is a killer," I said and closed the door behind me.

I was back at Peg's wagon in about fifteen seconds and knocking.

"It's me," I whispered.

"Toby?" she said. The wagon windows were dark.

"Yeah."

"I don't think it would work," her voice said, but there was no certainty in it.

"How do we know unless we try?" I pleaded.

"I'm not ready for something like this," she said.

"Let me in and we'll talk about it."

"No, you won't."

"Yes, I will," I said with comic emphasis.

She laughed, and a voice came booming from the next wagon, "Let him in, for Chrissake. I've got to get up at dawn and take care of fifteen horses."

She let me in.

chapter 10

Peg was right. It didn't work. I'm not sure what it was. Friendly but not comfortable. Touched but not moved. Friends. It wasn't what I had had in mind, but it wasn't bad either. There wasn't enough room in her bed for both of us to sleep. We tried for an hour, but my back began to ache again. She fell asleep while I was talking about the time I had been in New York chasing down a couple of runaway kids. I was in the Wellington Hotel across from the Waldorf. I thought the kids were in the room next to mine. I was going to wait till it got dark, knock at their door when they thought they were safe, and do my best to talk them into coming back to Los Angeles with me. I wasn't getting enough for the job to do anything else, and they were a pair of skinny little things with pimples who had some pretty good reasons for leaving home.

I had looked out of my window after taking a shower and seen something moving in the window of the Waldorf across the way at about the fifteenth or sixteenth floor. It was a small kid, maybe two years old, with red hair. He was leaning out of the open window. The wind was blowing, and I looked into the light of the room behind him or her for an adult to do something. There was no one there. I thought of calling the Waldorf desk, but I couldn't figure out what room it was, and by the time anyone got up there, the kid would be gone, one way or another. I thought of opening the window and yelling, but what would I yell even if the kid could hear me over the noise of the street? I might scare him into falling. But he was going to fall. No doubt about it. He or she put one foot up on the sill and looked down into the street.

I didn't know what to do. I couldn't decide whether to watch, run, close my eyes under the blankets, or pretend I wasn't seeing. I whispered to the kid to please crawl back. Then I stood there for maybe fifteen seconds watching until a figure behind the kid pulled him back and closed the window. The figure, a woman, turned her back, and the kid ran over to the bed in the room and that was all I could see. No one had suffered for what had happened in that room but me.

The pimply kids in the next room were laughing at Eddie Cantor on the radio when I knocked at their door a few minutes later. They opened it and asked what I wanted. They looked happy. I told them I had made a mistake, went to my room, packed, and headed back to L.A., where I told the parents that I couldn't find the kids.

Peg was asleep before I finished my story, which was fine with me because I wasn't sure of what the incident meant to me. If she had asked, I had no idea what I would tell her. I knew it was important. I knew I had thought about it a lot lately, and maybe that was enough. But Peg was asleep and so was my right arm, and my back ached again. So I crawled over her, took one of her two blankets and her extra pillow, and got on the floor. The floor was cool and hard and just what I wanted. To get rid of the little kid in the window, I thought about who my killer might be. That should have been enough to put me to sleep, but it was still early.

I listened to "Information Please" quietly on Peg's small Emerson while I tried to think. Boris Karloff and John Carradine were the guests, and they didn't get anything wrong. They knew that Jesse James was shot in the back of the head, that

Robin Hood was killed by someone letting his blood, and that Hamlet and Laertes were killed with poison rapiers. They were doing better with their fictional killers than I was doing with my real one.

It wasn't working. I kept thinking of dead aerialists, a red-haired kid in a window, and falling elephants. Sometimes the thing you least want to think about or imagine jumps in front of you like a clown in heat and won't go away: a disfigured man; some piece of rotten fish you ate when you were eight or nine; the memory of an elephant you never saw crumbling to the ground, landing on his knees and falling over dead.

For me the image that came now was Dr. Bumps. Dr. Bumps had been a small-time grifter on Broadway whose hand was barely steady enough to pick the pockets of bums and drunks and too-far-gones. Dr. Bumps had two big bumps on his forehead, like horns just starting to form or cut off because he had once too often gored someone on a streetcorner.

Dr. Bumps's head always hurt, and he let anyone who would listen to him know just how much it hurt, how much the images inside were taking form and "bumping to get out." You see, Dr. Bumps was convinced that anything he thought of could become real in his head, and if he didn't get rid of the image, it could expand and kill him. So he spent most of his time in pain thinking of ways to distract himself from thinking about anything he could imagine. It's hard to make a living, even as lousy a one as he made, while you fight a battle in your head. Dr. Bumps lost the battle in the spring of 1939. I don't know what he thought was growing in his head, but it was too much for him. He went down to Union Station, waited for an eastbound to Chicago, and jumped in front of it before it cleared the yard.

We found out, when Jeremy Butler and I went to identify the body, that Dr. Bumps's real name was Roland LeClerc III.

Was there an elephant growing in my head? Dr. Bumps looked over my shoulder from the past and told me there was. I wasn't going to argue with a dead nightmare.

I found a box of Kix by moonlight and filled a bowl. There

was a bottle of milk in Peg's ice chest under the window and a hot plate in the corner. I think the milk was slightly sour. I used it anyway and felt better with my stomach full.

When I'd finished my cereal someone knocked at the door, a small, I-don't-want-to-intrude knock. I opened the door and let Emmett Kelly in.

"I saw Elder down at the mess tent," he explained, stepping in. He was wearing a plaid flannel shirt and overalls and looked like an undersized lumberjack.

I offered him a seat and a cup of coffee. He took both and sat down with a lot of what was on his mind showing in his sun-browned face.

"You never really told me about that attempt on your life," I whispered, filling his coffee cup to the top. "It might help."

He looked relieved, as if that was what he had come for, and glanced at Peg to be sure she was asleep. I knew what he really wanted. I'd seen it on faces before. He wanted me to put the world back together.

"Well," Kelly began, looking at the wall as if the story he was about to tell would appear like a movie, "we were just setting up. Few days back. It's always the same, but there's something nice about it being the same. Like it was like this maybe a hundred years ago and it'll be there a hundred years from now even if people drop bombs on each other, rocket up to Mars, or dig a tunnel through the middle of the earth. Know what I mean?"

"Yes," I said, understanding but not really understanding. I believed it, but I didn't feel it. I wasn't part of anything like that, hadn't felt it about my family, the Glendale police, or Warner Brothers when I had worked for them. There was just me and today and maybe tomorrow and that wasn't so bad. In fact, it was usually pretty good, but it wasn't the kind of thing Kelly was part of.

"So anyway," he went on, taking his eyes from the movie that didn't appear on the wall and turning them to me for an instant before looking down at the coffee cup in his hand. The top of his head was nearly bald, and I had the feeling that I could see the past in it but not the future. "Anyway, the tents were going up, wagons coming in, mud all over. There's chicken rank in the circus, especially a runaround one like this one. Everybody's worried about who's higher in the coop, even some of us who've been around. I mean, we go year to year, and sometimes it stops for us. I've seen it. One year an act has it, the towners laugh, scream, clap their hands red. Next year, the magic is gone. No one knows for sure why. Maybe something inside you goes, jumps to someone else, goes no place particular. I mean, the circus goes on, but you don't. You slip, lose it. Happened to me when I was doing the high act. Hanging by my teeth one night spinning around maybe fifty feet up without a net, I knew it was gone. I mean, I was never a great one up there, but I wasn't bad. It just went. You can't hold it in. The other thing—Willie—had always been in me. I mean, he might just walk away someday, but I don't think so. I don't think we'd get on without each other. Am I making sense?"

I nodded. He made sense. Hell, there were all kinds of clowns in me. When I let them out, they usually caused me trouble. One clown in me wouldn't shut up when I was with my brother; the clown just jabbed and prodded with a word to the body and then another combination to the heart and cheek, and my brother would smash my nose or arm or leg. I knew that clown of mine.

"So," said Kelly with a smile at me as if he knew about my inner clown, "where was I? Oh, yes. Everybody worries about where they stand, but we all help out, especially in a put-together show for an old friend like Elder. I think I was helping to tie the canvas on a side tent. My hands were cold in the morning, and the sweat was sticking my shirt to my back. A guy named Gus the Gus, big Dane, was pulling with me when someone called. I turned around, didn't see anybody looking at me. The guy in the ticket booth had lost a roll of tickets, and they were unwinding and rolling downhill toward a puddle of mud. Gus the Gus could hold the rope. I patted him on the back, and with his face all red, he nodded that I could go. So

I took off to help catch the tickets. It was like a Mickey Mouse cartoon. Kept expecting the tickets to have one of those cartoony faces, get up on two painted legs and run away. Well, I didn't really, but you know."

I nodded again. I knew he was telling a story, and I wanted to be a good audience. Lots of reasons. I liked him. He was paying me, and he might have something that would help me.

"Well, I passed the ticket guy," said Kelly. "He's little and rickety, former Shetland pony act, I think. I was gaining on the tickets, going down that little hill, and figured I'd get them before they hit the puddle when I had that kind of itchy feeling, you know, hot rash on the neck when things are going warm when they should be cool. I turned and saw the truck. It was coming behind me, a small rigging truck, red, designed specially for circus jobs. At first I figured he was trying to help catch the tickets, which was a pretty damn silly thought. But I couldn't figure where else he was going."

"You didn't see anyone in the truck, a driver?" I tried.

Kelly looked back at the wall for a picture, touched his nose with his right forefinger, rubbed it and saw something.

"What did you see?" I pushed gently.

He shook his head. "Don't know," he said, moving his right hand down to rub his chin. "Have a sort of feeling there was a round something, like a balloon or a face or the moon. I didn't really look up there. I just kept running and running harder when I heard that truck right behind me. I remember thinking that the damned fool was going to run me down, and those tickets weren't worth my life."

Kelly looked at me to see if I was making sense out of this or thinking he was imagining things. I looked blank and straight without blinking so he'd go on, which he did.

"Anyway, the tickets went in the mud, and I leaped over the puddle and did a flying side roll to the left. Hadn't done one of those in almost ten years. Felt my side pull and hit a pile of Indian clubs a juggling act was unpacking. The truck went right by. I was rolling around in the clubs, but I watched it go. Missed me by no more than a foot, and there was no driver anymore, if there'd been one in the first place."

"Did you ask anyone if they had seen who started the truck?" I asked, reaching over for my cup. The cup was heavy and clean. Lots of things in this circus were heavy, clean, and repainted. I figured things were heavy so they wouldn't get destroyed in all the moving, and clean because the circus people didn't want to feel any shabbier than an Arab bandit life forced them to be.

"No luck," said Kelly, getting up to pour me coffee from the metal pot brewing on the hot plate. I watched the cloud of steam rise, put my hand over it and felt the moist circle of heat touch me.

"Gus the Gus had been holding the rigging, hadn't looked back. Ticket guy had his eyes on the tickets. Nobody saw. Nobody knew."

"Then that's about it for now," I said. "I'll pick up on it in the morning."

"OK," said Kelly, getting up to scratch his legs. "See you in the morning." He went out, closing the door gently behind him.

Whatever dreams I had were gone by morning except for one picture, Alfred Hitchcock near the lion cage. I remembered that he had been near the cage when I had talked to Henry the keeper. There was some chance that he had seen whoever had let the lion out or seen someone suspicious near the cage. After all, it had happened between the time I had talked to Henry and the start of the show, not too long, maybe fifteen minutes.

I got up quietly. My watch said it was nine, but I knew better than to listen to my watch. Hitchcock might have left, but I might be able to find the name of the friend in Mirador he was staying with. Even if I didn't, I could call him in Los Angeles. I also wanted a talk with Agnes Sudds about her failure to encounter Puddles in the supply tent.

There was no need to be quiet. Peg was gone. There was a note on the small table:

*DAY STARTS EARLY FOR ME. IF YOU MISS
BREAKFAST, MAKE SOME COFFEE. FRIENDS?*
PEG

My back felt reasonable. My clothes looked as if they had
been rolled into a ball and jumped on by a bear, and my face
looked no better in Peg's small mirror. I found her Ipana tooth-
paste, "For the smile of health." I rubbed it on with my fingers
and rinsed. The smile belonged to a healthy gargoyle.

Shoes on, I went out to face the day regardless of what time
it was. On the way to Kelly's wagon I passed people, but they
weren't giving out anything more than gloom and polite gri-
maces. A double death in the circus was nothing that could be
hidden.

Shelly was the only one in the wagon when I got there.

"Where are the others?" I said, rummaging through my
cardboard suitcase obtained three years earlier as payment for
a very small job from a very fat pawnbroker.

Shelly was at the table drinking coffee. He wasn't completely bald. A patch of hair touched each side of his head. The
hair on the right side was pointed out, making him look like a
mad professor in a Monogram horror picture for kids.

"They went back to find the people they're supposed to be
watching," he said, staring glumly into his cup. "I'm thinking
of going back home, Toby. Mildred said one night was all right.
And I've got Mr. Stange this afternoon. And Mrs. Ramirez . . ."

I found my razor, put in a fresh Blue Blade, and took off
my shirt. "I understand, Shel," I said, lathering the thin bar of
soap in a dish of cool water. And I did understand. Fun is fun,
but sleeping on a cot after a lion almost kills you isn't fun.

"Toby, I have some very important work to finish before . . ."

"Before you get killed in a circus," I continued, trying not
to cut my throat while I watched both it and Shelly's reflection
in the mirror. "Shel, you're not going to get killed here."

He shrugged, having little faith. "My profession . . ." he started but didn't know how to finish.

Fortunately, his profession took a turn for the better. Kelly came rushing in, dark jacket, green turtleneck sweater and all traces of Willie the Clown gone. "You're a dentist?" he asked Shelly.

"Right," said Shel, without looking up.

"We've got an emergency, a really bad tooth," said Kelly.

Shelly didn't look terribly interested. "I've got to get back to Los Angeles," he said, his eyes blinking behind his thick glasses. He fished into his jacket pocket and found the stub of a cigar. I could smell it when it reached the air even before he lit it.

"It's an emergency," said Kelly evenly and earnestly. "I know money won't make a difference, but we can pay fifty dollars if you'll just take a look and try to do something."

Professional pride welled in Shelly's face. "Emergency," he mused. "Well, let's get to it."

I finished shaving while Shelly told Kelly that he would have to go to his car for the emergency supplies he carried with him. By that I assumed he meant the small box of extra rusted tools he was always planning to pawn but could never get a decent price for unless three bucks was a decent price.

"What's the trouble?" asked Shelly, following Kelly, who opened the door for him to urge him out.

"Hurt her tooth last night when she got out, bit something probably, or someone," said Kelly.

Shelly stopped, put a hand on the wall. "The lion?" he gasped.

"Right," said Kelly, stepping down. "Puddles."

I rubbed the water and soap off of my face with a towel someone else had used earlier and went behind Shelly. "Can't let these people down, Shel," I whispered and gave him a solid shove through the door.

He stumbled, and Emmett Kelly caught him. I could see Shelly open his mouth to cry or protest. His hand went up to his head and touched his fringe of hair. Now both fringes had points, and he looked less like a mad dentist than a clown.

"How's the lion tamer?" I asked Kelly.

"He'll live," said Kelly, guiding Shelly down the path between the wagons, "but he might be a popcorn salesman from here on."

"Maybe he'll become a clown," I laughed.

"No," said Kelly seriously, a firm hand on Shelly's shoulder. "He isn't serious enough to be a good clown."

Shelly turned his head to me for help, and I waved at him with a smile. I put my second shirt on and my suit jacket, which was brown and didn't match my blue pants, but my windbreaker was bloody and gone, and I had no choice, unless I wanted to get back into the clown getup.

By asking a few questions of a chubby woman in a blue robe and curlers supporting her few strands of orange hair, I found out where Agnes Sudds and Abdul were making camp. By herself, the chubby woman told me confidentially. No one wanted to share space with the snakes. The chubby woman said she herself had nothing against snakes, but snake people were near the bottom of the circus social rung. Snakes were sideshow stuff, not big top. The chubby woman had a dog act, she told me, though I hadn't asked. I really didn't have to. I could smell it. The circus was full of smells that betrayed people.

Gunther was standing about forty feet from the wagon of Agnes Sudds when I came near. He was talking to two other people, a man and a woman who were even smaller than he was. I walked over to them, and the conversation stopped.

"This," said Gunther properly as always, "is my friend Mr. Peters. Toby, this is Fran and Anton Lieber. We worked together once in . . ."

"Madrid . . ." supplied Fran, who had a little-girl voice but the face of experience.

"We also worked together in *The Wizard of Oz* movie," added Anton.

Gunther's memory of that movie was not a fond one. I shook hands with both Anton and Fran. They had obviously been talking little-people talk, which I didn't think was anything different from big-people talk, but they were of a fraternity made by God or Darwin, and I wasn't.

"She is in the wagon," Gunther said to me, taking a step away from the Liebers after I had taken my leave of them.

"OK, I'll keep an eye on her for a while. See if you can track down Alfred Hitchcock. He's probably left, but he may be staying with someone in Mirador. I sure as hell can't go to Mirador with any questions."

"I understand," said Gunther. I noticed that he had changed clothes. He now wore a gray three-piece suit with a perfectly starched shirt and an immaculate pink tie and matching handkerchief in his pocket. He turned and moved back to his friends, and I walked boldly up to the wagon decorated with a snake painting that started with the head at the door and went around to the left, circling the entire wagon and emerging on the right side. The tail was a rattle, and the open-mouthed head was a warning, but I knocked, and Agnes Sudds's voice told me to come in.

It took a moment for my eyes to adjust to the darkness. The shades over the two wagon windows were thick and drawn. A small lamp was on, but the bulb was just a few watts and painted over in brown.

"Sorry," came Agnes' voice. "Some of the guys don't like a lot of light. It puts them to sleep."

I stood until I could see her figure in the corner near an open trunk. Then I could see that the trunk was a cage. Then I could see that Agnes wasn't alone. A large, thick snake was draped around her waist and over her shoulder, and she was stroking its head.

Agnes was dressed in a gray sweat shirt and trousers. Her red hair, red like that of the kid in the window of the Waldorf, was tied with a ribbon and hanging down her back. She looked cute, a little like Lucille Ball. Or she would have looked cute if it weren't for the snake, who looked like the one painted on the wagon.

"Murray," she said, smiling and stroking the snake. "His

name is Murray. You want to make friends?"

"No, thanks," I said. "I mean, you and I, yes, but Murray and I can stay cordial."

"Cordial," she repeated. "Education and everything. Snakes feel good. Cool, friendly, soothing. Holding a snake is very restful. They like being near warm bodies."

"That a fact?" I said with a smile. "How's Abdul?"

"Resting," she said, putting a finger to her lips to indicate that we had to be quiet. I wondered where Abdul-the-green might be resting. In some corner of the room? Above me? I decided to make the visit short.

"Have a seat," she said, still standing.

"I'm comfortable," I said. "Murray posed for the picture on your wagon?"

"No," she said, rolling her eyes upward at my stupidity. "Murray is a python. The picture is a rattlesnake. Rattlesnakes are not friendly. But it makes a nice picture on the wagon. You know. Identifies me. Like Charlie McCarthy and Chase and Sanborn."

"I see," I said, looking around for Abdul and others of his ilk. The wagon was small and the neatest one I had yet seen in the circus, even neater than Peg's. It was decorated in restful browns made more brown by the painted bulb. The walls were paneled in wood, with one wall of small cages filled with grass in which, I was sure, lurked slithering snakes.

My hand reached out and touched something cold against the other dark wall, and I pulled it away. I had touched a cage, and something had rustled inside it.

Agnes laughed gently. "Those are frogs," she said. "I keep dozens of them."

"You have a frog act too?" I asked.

"No, I feed the frogs to Murray and some of the others."

Murray looked at me and seemed to yawn. He had clearly never seen as stupid a human as I was.

"Can I do something for you?" Agnes said with something that might have been interpreted as seductive. "Or is Peg doing everything you need? But Peg can't be doing very much." She crinkled her nose like Shirley Temple. "Peg is the circus good girl."

"And you're the circus bad girl?" I said, trying to stay in the middle of the room and glancing up at the ceiling a few feet over my head.

"Not bad, exactly," she said. "Mina, she works with the horses. Now that's a bad girl. I'm just average bad, if you like average bad."

"I like information," I said. "I'll talk about degrees of badness later. Would you mind putting Waldo back in his bed while we talk?"

"His name is Murray," she said, looking into the snake's rheumy eyes. "He needs affection or he gets leathergic."

"I think that's lethargic," I corrected. "OK, I'm a little curious about why you and Abdul didn't spot Puddles in that tent last night. It isn't a very big tent, and he's a very big lion."

"*She's* a very big lion," Agnes corrected me as she began to untangle Murray gently from her body. "I don't know. Maybe she was scared and just being quiet. Maybe she circled around behind me. Maybe Abdul scared her, or she came under the tent as I was leaving. Why?"

Murray was almost unwound, and Agnes began to coax him into the trunk. She cooed to him while waiting for my answer.

"You didn't like Rennata Tanucci," I said. "Her husband liked you. Someone might think you had a reason to want to get rid of both of them. First the husband, maybe because he was going back to his wife, and then the wife because you resented giving him up."

Murray was safely back in the box when Agnes locked the trunk and turned her eyes on me. I expected hate or anger. I was trying to provoke her, but she looked amused.

"I turned him down," she said, lifting her chin. "I don't need to chase flyers. Plenty of men in this circus know a class act when they see one." She put her hand on her hip and looked at me with a smile. I couldn't make out much of her body under the sweat suit, but she was reminding me of what I had seen the day before.

"How long have you been with the circus?" I asked.

The hand came off the hip. "What's that got to do with it?" she asked with some of the amusement gone.

"Hey," I said. "I'm trying to find a killer. I'm trying to eliminate people. I'm doing a job. If I can eliminate enough people, what I'll be left with is a killer. There might be an easier way, but I don't know easier ways."

"The Thin Man doesn't work like that," she sneered.

"He has a script and a smart wife."

"And a dog," she added.

"And a dog," I agreed. Then there was silence.

"I was with Sell-Floto for ten years," she said. "Just joined this one last month."

"And before that?" I pushed. Another silence.

"Five years with the Tom Mix Show, Helig's, others," she said, looking away. "I started when I was a real young kid."

"Right," I agreed. The frogs rustled behind me. "You happy in the circus?"

"I like the snakes, the ones without legs," she said with a smile.

"Must get to you after all this time to still be in a sideshow while people like the Tanuccis are under the big top, center ring. Even the lions and elephants get center ring."

Agnes laughed. I was surprised that I liked the laugh. The little-girl front cracked with that laugh. She shook her head.

"I'm not knocking off animals and people because I got dreams about dragging my snakes into the big top," she said. "Snakes don't drive you nuts. They soothe you. You learn from them. You learn to be perversive."

"Passive?" I tried.

"Very," she agreed. "Now, if you want to stop trying to nail me for murder and World War II, maybe we could be friends. I'd really like to know about private investigators. I listen to all the shows on the radio. Sam Spade, Sherlock Holmes, Richard Diamond, Nero Wolfe. I go to movies.

Charlie Chan at the Circus was one of my favorites. Nothing like the circus, but like what people think about it. You know?"

The little-girl interest was back, and I liked it. She sort of swayed from hip to hip as she talked, and I felt as if I were being hypnotized. Maybe it was just the darkness, the air in the wagon, and my knowing that snakes named Murray and Abdul and frogs that were going to be swallowed whole were all around me.

"Well," I said, "maybe we'll talk again soon." I backed to the door, reaching for the handle.

"Do you do anything besides talk?" she said, pursing her lips.

"We'll talk about it," I said and leaped out into the air, pushing the door closed behind me.

I breathed deeply and looked around. Gunther and his friends were nowhere around, so I headed toward the big top. Gunther intercepted me while I paused to watch a man about fifty walking behind three small boys in green tights and matching blue jackets. The man was shaking his head and shouting to them about looking straight ahead, always straight ahead.

"Funambulists," said Gunther, looking at the quartet as it passed us. "Rope walkers. Family tradition. The word comes from the Latin *funis*—rope—and *ambulare*—to walk. It goes back thousands of years. Some say the acrobats and rope walkers are the oldest tradition in the circus next to the clowns, if we acknowledge that the *commedia dell'arte* is, indeed, clearly a part of the circus tradition and not the theater."

"I acknowledge," I said. "What did you find out about Hitchcock?"

"He is here," Gunther said, still watching the receding figures of the rope walkers. "In the big tent, watching. The circus grapevine is fast, and outsiders are sensed like a low-level voltage. . . ."

"Shock," I said.

Gunther nodded, adding the word to his vocabulary.

"I suppose that includes me, that outside shock?"

"Yes," he said. "Your presence is felt. Mine is less so because I have been with a circus and for other reasons. Jeremy too, for some reason, is accepted, perhaps because of his wrestling and size. I'd best return to my duties outside the wagon of the reptile woman."

"Thanks, Gunther," I said and went into the big top.

There were streaks of sunlight coming through entrances to the tent and a central opening at the peak of the tent. Some of the lights were on, and people were practicing acts in various rings. In one side ring, the three Tanuccis were standing in a small group. The eldest Tanucci was pointing up to the trapeze and speaking earnestly.

In the center ring, a cage had been set up, a big animal cage, and inside it stood young Shockly and a tired tiger, looking at each other with mutual confusion, or so it seemed to me.

I looked around for Hitchcock, and Elder came to my side, his mustache trim and waxed, his scalp moist, his green sweater snug over his well-muscled chest and only the sag of a cheekbone revealing doubt.

"Tanuccis are trying to put a makeshift act together," he said. "We have to pull them from center ring, but when word gets out about the murder . . ."

"Murders," I corrected, but he went on.

"Murders," he agreed. "People will want to see them. Things like this have happened before. We pulled Shockly up from an apprenticeship to see if he can handle the cats. We've got no show without a cat act. My partner back East is trying to get Beatty, but he's hard to find. There's Grunwald in England. Retired. We might get him, but by the time he got here the season would be over and we'd be headed for a home run, headed back to Florida."

"Someone's doing a good job wrecking the circus," I observed, looking around for Hitchcock and spotting him sitting alone and placidly watching, his pudgy hands folded in his lap. He was dressed in a dark suit and seated several rows up in the wooden grandstands. "What's Hitchcock doing here?" I said.

"He asked to watch," replied Elder. "He's a well-known film producer, and he keeps his mouth shut. Maybe it will make some good publicity. Who knows?"

"He's a director," I corrected, moving toward Hitchcock.

"What's the difference?" said Elder, heading away without waiting for an answer.

Hitchcock looked up at me languidly while I climbed the stands. His eyes scanned my clothing. "Good morning," he said.

"Good morning," said I, sitting next to him but not too close.

"I do not wish to be rude," he said, looking back at the Tanuccis, "but your trousers and jacket do not match. Nor does your shirt."

"All I have left," I shrugged, watching the Tanuccis in their huddle.

"I think it essential that one dress carefully and formally when one works," he said. "It establishes the aura of seriousness necessary in a potentially chaotic situation."

"Maybe so," I sort of agreed. "But the world I work in doesn't seem to be affected by my sense of anything."

"The difference between life and movies," said Hitchcock. "I prefer movies. In fact, I have no great affection for the real world."

The Tanuccis were climbing the rope ladder to the trapeze, led by Carlo. In the center ring, Elder had entered the cage with Shockly and the tiger and was urging the kid on, saying something about how old the tiger was. The tiger seemed to be asleep.

"Absolutely fascinating," sighed Hitchcock.

"I thought you were going back to Los Angeles," I said.

"I am," said Hitchcock evenly. "My friend was good enough to put me up for another night so that I might discover something more of the events of the last day. You have not, I may presume, discovered a murderer or a motive?"

"Nope," I said, searching my pockets for something without knowing what, maybe Abdul the snake. Instead, I found a single peanut. I offered to share it with Hitchcock, who refused politely.

"Pity," he said. "I'll have to depart nonetheless. Might I suggest that you are searching for someone who is quite mad? When you discover the nature of that madness, the key to it, what obsession moves this man or woman, you will discover your killer."

"Great," I said, munching my peanut as the youngest surviving Tanucci, Tino, swung out on the trapeze. "Now all I need is a psychiatrist. You know a lion was let loose last night?"

"I am aware of that," he said, his eyes watching Tino without moving his head.

"You were near the cage just before it happened," I said, fishing some peanut from between my teeth.

Hitchcock glanced at me and made it clear, though he tried not to, that he did not approve of people picking their teeth in public. "May I assume, therefore," he said, "that I am a suspect?"

"No," I said. "You're not a suspect. You're a possible witness."

"I was rather hoping for something grander than that," he said, "but then it might mean an encounter with the police, a situation which I would do very nearly anything to avoid."

The Tanuccis were trying some switches and routines tentatively, with the older Tanucci shouting changes, suggestions in Italian, encouraging, discouraging, supporting.

"Did you see anybody near the cage?" I went on.

"The keeper who has such great difficulty with the human language," said Hitchcock, "and one other person, a woman. A red-haired woman with a gaudy costume. She stood beside me watching the lions. We exchanged no conversation."

Agnes again, thought I.

"I left before she did," he added. "There certainly may have been others. I left just in time to see the show."

"Well," I said, getting up, "I've got to get back to work."

Hitchcock put out his pudgy right hand, and I took it. It

was deceptively firm. "Perhaps we will encounter each other again," he said. "If you are in the directory, I may call you, if you have no objection."

"None," I said. "And thanks for the theory."

Elder was still trying to introduce the shy Shockly to the weary tiger when I went into the light. I'd have to talk to Agnes again, but I wasn't sure of how it would go. I didn't have enough to turn her over to Nelson, and I wasn't sure I could break her down. It would take a little thought. I headed for the animal tent. It was dark but full of sounds.

Gargantua eyed me lazily when I came in. He was standing and trying to see beyond the bars to whatever strange events were taking place to his left, just out of sight.

Peg and Shelly came toward me with the doctor. Behind them I could see Puddles lying in her cage while the other lion leaned over her with what looked like concern.

"Did he kill her?" I asked Peg, whose hair was down completely.

"Kill her?" said Shelly. "I saved that animal's jaw alignment. Filed down the left number three and evened them. Damn, Toby, wait till I report this to the county society."

"He did a good job," nodded the old doctor in what sounded like astonishment.

"He's used to working with animals," I said. "Puddles is probably one of the tamest patients Shelly's had in months."

"Just put her to sleep," said Shelly with a gloat. "Easiest thing I've done. I'd like some of that stuff to put my patients out."

"It'd kill a human," said the doctor.

"Well," gloated Shelly, "I could control it. Temper it, you know. Be careful."

"I'd advise against it," said Doc Ogle, but I could see Shelly considering a nice dose of whatever it was for Mrs. Ramirez and Mr. Stange. We would need a long talk at some point in the near future.

Shelly put an arm around the old doctor, who tried to shrink away, but Shelly wasn't having any. Cigar in mouth,

Shel was describing to the old man what he had done in terms which were far from technical.

"You see the way I sawed that damn thing down? Then all it took was the file and a tape measure. If you know what you're doing, it comes easy. Now, about that fifty dollars . . ."

Peg, at my side, took my arm. "I'm sorry about last night, Toby," she said. "It's just that I'm . . ."

I gave her a squeeze and suggested that we forget about it and find a killer. It seemed a good idea to both of us.

Peg had to locate Elder. I told her where he was and left Shelly oppressing the doctor. I headed back for Agnes Sudds's wagon, working out a plan. I didn't have one quite worked out when I got there. I seldom did, but as it turned out, I didn't need one.

I started to open the door to the wagon with the snake's face on it and heard a cry behind me.

"No, Toby," came Gunther's voice. I turned to face him as he stepped out from behind a nearby wagon, but it was too late.

"Ah, Mr. Peters," came a voice which was far from back home or friendly. "Perhaps you could just step in so we can settle a few things."

I considered running, but I knew I'd get a bullet in my back. The thought made my tender spine tingle. So I stepped into the wagon and grinned at Sheriff Nelson and Deputy Alex. Agnes stood back in the corner, drinking something clear and cool-looking.

"Venom?" I asked, glancing at her glass.

Agnes gave a nasty smirk. Alex and Nelson wouldn't even give that.

"You will hold out your hand," said Nelson, adjusting his dirty white hat with one hand and leveling his pistol at me with the other. "Alex will affix a handcuff to your wrist, and we will go back to Mirador on this lovely morning to have that little talk that was interrupted yesterday."

"She did it," I said, nodding at Agnes.

Nelson sighed enormously. "Your hand, Peters, or I shall be forced to shoot you before Alex has the opportunity for further discussion."

I looked at Alex, who touched his right hand to his neck. Maybe a quick bullet or two would be better than a few minutes with Alex.

Agnes, however, was more interested in what I was saying than what Nelson was going on about. "Me?" she said, plunking her now empty glass on the table. "I did it? I did what?"

"You had something to do with letting the lion out, probably the killings of the Tanuccis," I said evenly, holding out my wrist.

"You bastard," she shouted. Animals rustled throughout the room, and Nelson looked nervous.

"Now, just a minute," Nelson shouted. Alex clamped a cuff on my right hand and made it tight.

Agnes moved to the trunk where Murray resided.

"There's a python in there," I said to Nelson.

He turned to the trunk, gun outstretched. "It would be best if you didn't touch that," he said. "I'll blow a hole through you and it if I see any damn snake."

Agnes hesitated.

"She had something to do with it," I insisted.

"Then we shall just take her with us too," said Nelson, nodding to Alex. Alex dragged me across the small room to Agnes. He grabbed her arm and clamped the other end of the cuff to her wrist. Agnes and I were now hitched.

"Now," said Nelson, "we shall just leave quietly. I will brook no interference from the people here."

Agnes kicked me two or three times, and I told her softly that if she did it one more time I'd smash her face with my free left hand. She kicked me again, and I raised my fist.

"OK," she said, covering up.

Alex pulled us out the door and down the stairs. Outside, Gunther stood helplessly.

"Gunther," I said. "Find Elder. Tell him Agnes and I are being taken to Mirador. I'm not going to cause any trouble, and

I'd like a lawyer over there before anything happens to me."

"I understand," said Gunther.

"Call Marty Leib in L.A.," I shouted back as Alex prodded Agnes and me forward. "Maybe he knows some good local lawyer."

"I understand," he said sadly.

Nelson was sweating as he got into the back seat of the police car. I saw the scratch on the police car as I got in. I had done a bit of damage to the Mirador police department and was, I expected, about to suffer for it. Agnes and I were crowded into the front seat next to Alex, who drove. Nelson sat in the back seat with his gun leveled at us.

And off we went in the general direction of Mirador.

chapter 11

It was difficult to enjoy the scenery on the trip back to Mirador. On my left, Alex drove slowly, savoring what he was going to do to me when he got me alone. He gave my leg a loving squeeze. My brother had done that once when we were kids, and I had never forgotten the pain. Alex was going Phil one pain better. Behind me sat a now satisfied Mark Nelson humming, "Side By Side." At my right sat Agnes Sudds, who was more than angry with me for dragging her into this and accusing her of murder. I avoided Agnes for a while and tried to see Nelson's face in the rearview mirror.

"Sit still," warned Alex.

"My wrist hurts," I said.

"Alex will soon take your mind off that discomfort," said Nelson from the back seat. He had stopped singing "Side By Side" and had switched to the "Rickety Rickshaw Man."

"Doesn't bother you that I'm not the killer?" I said.

"Not a jot," beamed Nelson. "The two victims, or one that I am sure of, were not citizens of Mirador. They are from the outside, and their killer, who I assume to be you, is also from outside our tranquil confines. When the circus goes tomorrow, the killer goes too, if you are not the killer. However, you are the killer."

"You don't even really think I am," I said. "You just want this wrapped up."

"Like a Baby Ruth candy bar," he said.

"Why don't you tell him again that I did it?" hissed Agnes like one of her snakes.

I was about to suggest just that when I looked at Agnes. I didn't like the way she was smiling or the way she looked down toward her lap. I looked down at her lap too and saw Abdul curled there, gazing at me.

"Holy . . ." I said with nowhere to go but through the windshield. I couldn't even do that without taking Agnes and Abdul with me.

"What the hell is wrong with you, Peters?" said Nelson.

"The snake," I said calmly.

"Snake? What the hell are you jaw-flapping about? You hit the bottle this morning?"

"In her lap," I whispered to Alex.

He looked toward her lap and saw the snake.

"Coral snake," Agnes said sweetly. "You'll be dead in seconds if Abdul strikes."

"Listen, Agnes . . ." I began, looking from Alex's suddenly white knuckles on the steering wheel to Agnes' eyes of green fire.

"What is going on up there?" complained Nelson, holding his gun up. "Alex, watch the damn road, and you two be quiet."

"What would I do now if I was the killer?" Agnes said between clenched teeth.

I had the insane vision of my high school English teacher, Miss Routt. We called her Rutt. She prodded me to tell Agnes that she should use the conditional tense. "If I were," I said to myself.

"I'd let Abdul sink his clean little fangs into your dirty leg," she said. "But I'm not the killer."

"I think I believe you," I said.

"We all believe you, lady," said Alex emotionlessly. He

was weaving back and forth on the road. Nelson said something like "What the hell" and leaned over into the front seat to see what was going on. He saw Abdul and let out a yell. His gun went off, turning the windshield milky white and full of threads before it crumpled inward. Alex lost control, and the car turned sharply to the right. Nelson tumbled into the front seat as Abdul went flying into the air. I saw a green streak go past my nose through the window. I think I was upside down at the time.

Colors were flying together like blood or oil in a pool of water. A noise of metal against metal against metal against me stopped or almost stopped. Something was still grinding slowly. The car engine was turning over.

Someone was on top of me. From the weight, I knew it was Alex. I pushed and pushed with my free left hand until something gave way, and Alex floated upward, which surprised me until I decided that the car and I were upside down. My foot was through the roof.

"Nelson," I croaked, looking around, but I didn't see him.

"He went through the front window," said Agnes below me. We were still handcuffed together. "Abdul is out there too."

"Are you hurt?" I asked.

"I don't think so," she said, getting to her knees. "Is the deputy dead?"

Alex was breathing evenly, and his eyes were fluttering. He didn't look great, but he didn't look dead or near it.

"I think he's just stunned," I said. "How about pulling me down gently? My leg went through the roof."

We worked at it for a few seconds, and I came tumbling down. Alex broke my fall and groaned.

"Come on," I said to Agnes, opening the car door. It creaked and slumped open. She followed me out.

"It will be easier if we hold hands," I suggested. "The cuffs won't rub us raw." I took her reluctant hand. It felt comforting. Maybe Nelson, if he was alive, would hesitate to shoot us if we simply stood holding hands in the road.

"Let's look for Abdul," Agnes whimpered. "The poor thing is out of his native environment and friendless."

"You just described Tobias Leo Pevsner," I said. "Me."

We found Nelson sprawled on a grass embankment about ten feet from the car. The gun was gone, and he was sitting and holding his head.

"Alex," he groaned. "Where the hell is my hat?" He looked up at us standing in the road, and blurry hatred appeared. "I am going to find my gun and blast a hole in two escapees," he vowed. On his knees like a mad animal, he began to scramble around, searching for gun, hat, and, possibly, Abdul.

"I think we better get the hell out of here," I told Agnes.

She looked at the frenzied Nelson and nodded in agreement.

"Nelson, we didn't kill anybody," I said, hurrying down the road, across it, and toward a clump of trees.

"Stop," he shouted, postponing his search and getting to his wobbly legs. He took a step toward us and toppled over. My last look back showed me Alex crawling out of the wreck. We ran through bushes, trees, scrub, and stones. No bullets followed us. I wouldn't have heard footsteps over my own heavy breathing even if they were there. We ran and ran. I prayed for Agnes of a Thousand Snakes to ask for a rest. That was the way it was supposed to go, but she wasn't even breathing hard.

"OK." I stopped. "That's it. I need a rest. You win."

"You should stay in good condition," she said.

"I thought I was." I looked back the way we had come, but there was no sound and no sight of pursuit. We had done some zigzagging, and now I was sagging. I staggered to a rock that looked like a buried brown egg and leaned against it.

"Congratulations," I said. "I think you just introduced the coral snake to Southern California. He'll be right at home."

Agnes looked at me coldly. "Tell me something," she said. "Why the hell am I running?"

"Easy," I said, trying not to sound winded because she didn't. "You're handcuffed to me and I'm running. If we can get you loose, you can run right back to those two. They're going to have some questions about Abdul, me, and a couple of murders."

"I didn't murder anybody," she screamed.

After pleading with her to keep her voice down, I went over her story. Actually, she didn't have a story, just answers to my questions, and they were pretty good answers, which meant I was getting confused. I was also getting worried. Alex or Nelson could come crashing through the trees, guns ablaze, any second.

"So what do we do?" Agnes asked reasonably. "Where do we go?"

"That way," I nodded, "and then south. They expect us to head north up the coast toward Los Angeles. Nelson will probably look for us himself for a few hours and then call in the state police. He won't want to call them in, but maybe he'll have to. They already know he's an idiot. Then I'll have to think of something. Like who the hell the killer is."

"You don't know what you're doing, do you?" she said reasonably.

"Of course I do," I said, pushing away from the rock, my right hand still clutching her left. "I'm wearing a jacket that doesn't match my pants, holding the hand of a snake charmer in a sweat shirt, and running away from a sheriff who wants to blow my head off. How many people in the world can be that specific about what they're doing?"

We went more slowly, but we didn't stop until we came to a ridge. About fifty feet below us were jagged rocks, and just beyond them were the beach and ocean. There was no path, but there was enough brush to hold onto as we made our way down, which wasn't very easy with one free hand each. Once Agnes slipped and let go of my hand. The cuffs cut into our wrists but kept her from going backwards while I clung to a rock. When we finally made it to the beach, we were both exhausted.

"Do you do things like this a lot?" she said.

"Not a lot, but it happens," I admitted, looking out at the waves.

"Am I nuts, or do you look like you're having a good time?"

"Maybe not exactly a good time," I said, "but it beats sitting in the front room, reading the *Times* and watching the clock take your life away. I'm scared a lot, but I'm alive more than other people too."

"Like snakes," Agnes said sympathetically. "You know what they can do, and that's why you want to be with them, show other people you can be that near death and like it."

"Kindred spirits," I said, helping her up.

She stood looking into my battered face with an amused smile. I kissed her nose.

"Your name really Sudds?" I asked as we started down the beach, walking on stones to keep from leaving prints.

"Would anyone make up a name like that?" she said. "It's Sudds. In my act, I'm Helene of Nepal, whose parents were killed by bandits during an exploring trip of Tibet. I was brought up by snake worshippers and became their princess, but I found their sacrifices of travelers to the snake god repellent and escaped to a Jesuit missionary."

"And people buy that?"

"No," she admitted, "but they like to pretend they do or make fun of it. They mainly like to see someone doing something they wouldn't dare do. That's the story of the circus."

We kept walking, did a little talking and a lot of thinking, but the thinking wasn't getting me anywhere. If I went back to the circus with Agnes, it would probably be knee deep in state police by nightfall. If I went to Los Angeles, I'd have nothing to work with. I'd be picked up in a few hours. If I went to Mirador, I wouldn't even get a chance to explain.

After an hour of walking, we came to a few houses and a pier. Not much of a pier, a concrete breaker worn away by the ocean. There was a path up from the beach and we took it, holding hands and hiding the cuffs under my baggy jacket sleeve. We were two ridiculously dressed lunatics in love if anyone saw us. If our description had gotten to this town already, there would be no denying it. Our disguise was only for the indifferent or uninformed. I had a few dollars in my wallet, not enough to buy our way out of this but enough for coffee and a few sinkers.

The houses, old adobe and cracking wood, came closer and closer together until we got to what passed for downtown. The smell of the ocean helped make the place seem more quaint than decaying. It certainly wasn't full of activity.

A few signs in store windows let us know that we were in Quiggley, California. The grocery store and post office, which also had a soda fountain, displayed a sign that told us Quiggley was "The Fifth Leading Producer of Artichokes in Southern California."

A few farm kids were sitting at the fountain drinking Green Rivers. They looked at us, poked each other, and made it clear that they were holding back giggles.

"Finish up and off you go," said a woman behind the counter. She was gray from hair to smock and as thin as string. With a see-what-the-world-has-done-to-me little smile, she asked us what we wanted. I ordered coffee for both of us and some doughnuts.

"Got some fresh-made pecan rolls," said the woman.

"Sounds fine," I said, giving Agnes a loving look to account for our tightly held hands.

"Renting a place down by the beach?" the woman said, moving slowly to get our order.

"Right," I said. "Just a few days. Place a few miles up the coast. We just strolled down to see what Quiggley was like."

"And?" asked the woman, reaching to turn on the radio behind her next to a metal sign with a picture of a smiling girl holding up a Coke bottle to the sun.

"It's nice," said Agnes, looking around the store.

The place was old, cluttered, and full of the smell of moist wood. I liked it. The radio suddenly warmed up, and Dr. I.Q.'s voice came on with a question: "For ten silver dollars," he said, filled with enthusiasm, "where is the Island of Kwato?"

"New Guinea," said Agnes, trying to figure out a way of splitting her pecan roll with one hand. "There's a little blue snake in Kwato that turns itself upside down to get its vemon out."

"That a fact?" said the woman behind the counter. Agnes dipped the whole pecan roll in the coffee.

"The Caribbean," said a woman on the radio, and Dr. I.Q. responded with his, "I'm awfully sorry. The Island of Kwato is part of New Guinea, but a box of Milky Ways to that lady."

A couple of women came in to buy stamps, and I urged Agnes to hurry. She did, and I left half a buck on the counter. We didn't wait for change.

"See you," I said pleasantly as we walked around a display of Uneeda Biscuits for ten cents a box.

The gray woman and the stamp customers looked over at us, and I heard one of their voices say, "Strange, Walter says spies are . . ." Behind them, Dr. I.Q. started a tongue twister that began, "My mother's monkey makes . . ."

"I'm still hungry," said Agnes as we went down the street. We would soon be out of the town, and I had no plan, just some wild ideas that made no sense. In short, my usual state. A brown car pulled around a corner and headed toward us. There were a few cars on the main street of Quiggley which was, not surprisingly, called Main Street. This car, however, had a little light on the top.

We were standing near a lawn in front of a small wooden building marked RR Station. I didn't know if it was still in use or what call Quiggley had for a railroad, but I pulled Agnes toward the door. It opened easily, and we stepped in. I looked back through the dingy window of the door to watch the police car go past.

Someone was in the station. I didn't look. Instead, I walked to the blackboard I spotted at the corner of my eye, pulling Agnes with me. It told what trains were coming and going through Quiggley. There weren't many. The next one out was to Phoenix at three in the morning.

"If anyone asks," I whispered, "we're going to Phoenix and we've already got our tickets."

"And no luggage," said Agnes. We sat on a wooden bench.

I looked down as if I were tired and saw blue linoleum squares with white flecks. The linoleum was scuffed and worn through to dirty wood in spots. The walls were covered with plaster put on in uneven layers and painted over gray-white like a strip mine.

There was a young man behind the ticket booth in the corner. From what I could see of him, he had a dark mustache and hair Wildrooted to submission. The black lettering on the pebbled glass above his booth had worn or been scratched away so that only "TI KE S" remained. The radiators were old, ornate, and painted black. A black-on-white sign above the door we had come through said, "No Loitering." There were some gray steel lockers and a few windows painted over at the top in flecked black. The wooden benches were high-backed. The garbage can in the corner was full, as was the ashtray a few feet from us.

We weren't the only customers waiting. An Oriental family shared the station and drew most of the looks of the ticket taker. The father and the pregnant mother looked young. She was lying on the bench with her eyes closed. The father, a thin man in a denim jacket, looked at us with a small apologetic smile. All four of the kids had running noses. The oldest was about seven. The father clutched a small radio in his arms.

One of the kids walked over to Agnes and me. He was about six and carrying a crumpled Captain Marvel comic book. His black hair tumbled over his eyes.

"We're Chinese," he said, "not Japanese."

"Great," I said. "What's your name?"

"Miles," he said and then whispered, "but my real name is Tetsuya."

I wasn't sure of my Oriental names, but I didn't think Tetsuya was Chinese. What he was, was the product of his father and mother's real fear. They were on the run and probably didn't know where they were heading, as long as it was away from California and the camps where Japanese-Americans were being herded.

"My real name is Tobias," I said, holding out my left hand.

My right hand was otherwise occupied holding Agnes and hiding handcuffs.

Miles took my hand, shook it, and informed us that a nickel was stuck in the public telephone in the corner. His brothers and sister climbed the benches and gradually made their way to us. I wondered, while exchanging silly looks with them, what would happen when Agnes or I had to go to the rest room. At one point, Agnes glanced at the ladies' room. I ignored her and my own bladder and played with the kids. The father looked worried, and I had the impression that the pregnant mother was only pretending to be asleep.

After an hour or so, two of the kids fell asleep. Miles went to the telephone with the remaining brother to work on the nickel, and I ignored Agnes and the eyes of the ticket taker by picking up a movie magazine. The magazine had the cover torn off, and I didn't really want to know about the Stage Door Canteen shows, but I flipped the pages slowly, as if reading them. Agnes dozed, waiting for me to come up with an idea, and then the idea came up with me. It was on the page right in front of me.

"Son of a . . ." I began.

"What?" Agnes said droopily.

I stuffed the magazine in my pocket, pulled Agnes to her feet, and hurried to the door.

"Where are we going?" she said.

"I've got some answers and ideas," I said. "Let's go." I waved left-handed to Miles and his brother and hurried Agnes out into the day.

"Back to Mirador," I said. "I think I have some evidence for the state police."

We didn't want to go back to the gray lady's grocery and post office, so we stopped at the town diner, where we caught a suspicious look or two, bought a few Whiz bars, and headed back to the beach.

"I need a bathroom," Agnes said as I hurried her along away from the last touches of Quiggley civilization.

"So do I," I said, "but . . ."

"Bushes, eyes closed," she said. "Now."

The rest of the walk, all two hours plus of it, gave me Agnes' real life story. I didn't listen to most of it, just nodded, smiled when it seemed right and kept on going, trying to make sense of what I knew. It was late in the afternoon when I recognized the stretch of beach where I had last seen the running elephant. Another two hundred yards and we were at the spot where I had found Rennata Tanucci's body.

"What kind of place is this?" Agnes asked, looking around at the unfinished buildings.

"Ghost town," I said. "Let's get up there and get some help."

We climbed the road and went to the first house on the ridge overlooking the beach. It was a two-story brown brick place in this, the classier part of town near the ocean. The grounds were well maintained, and the wall was low and matching brick. It would have a phone, and it might have a reasonable owner of some position in Mirador, someone who might mediate between Agnes and me and the law. The sun was setting on the horizon, and the first chill of February night roared by when I knocked at the oak door. There was a light on upstairs, so I knocked again. Then the footsteps came, heavy and slow, and the door opened.

There is good luck and bad luck and no luck at all. I never knew which would be there when a door opened. This time it opened on the double-faced Thomas Paul.

"Mr. Peters," he said. "To what do I owe this surprise?"

There wasn't much choice, and besides, I was pretty sure now who my murderer was, so I took the chance.

"Your sheriff is after us for murder," I said.

"Yes, I know," he said. "The young woman down on the beach. Won't you come in?" He stepped back, and I led Agnes in behind me.

The hallway was dark, but the last of the sunlight was enough to see by as we followed Paul to the right and into a living room. The furniture was comfortable, soft and dark, and the walls were covered with paintings, circus paintings: clowns, jugglers, aerialists, elephants, even a band.

"I told you I wanted the circus in Mirador," said Paul, watching my face. "I have deep feelings for the circus, deep feelings. And you, young lady, you are Helene, the charming snake charmer. I saw your act yesterday."

"I saw you seeing my act yesterday," said Agnes, sitting on a sofa and pulling me down with her.

Paul's right hand went up to his face. "Yes," he said, "I'm rather difficult to miss. Now, what can I do for you? As you know, I want to make relations with the circus as cordial as possible. I cannot, however, harbor killers."

"Accused killer," I said. "I know who the real killer is, and I can prove it."

Paul looked at me with one side smiling and the other side of his face twisted in what looked like hatred. "Good," he said. "I'd like this settled, and I don't want any trouble. Can I get you something to eat and perhaps a file or saw?"

"Great, and get the state police here," I said.

"Make yourselves comfortable," replied Paul, walking out the door and closing it behind him. "I'll take just a few minutes."

"Up," I said. She sighed, pouted, and got to her weary feet. We walked on the Persian carpet to the rear of the room, to a wide bay window that looked down at the beach. I could see the spot where Rennata had been killed and Nelson had found me over the body.

"Don't you wonder why he closed the door behind him when he walked out?" I said.

"No," she answered. "He said he's getting the state cops and a file. That's all I care about."

"He didn't say that. I asked him to do it, but he didn't say he would. Come on."

We went to the door of the living room, and I opened it. I could hear Paul's voice at the back of the house through another closed door. We followed the sound, walking softly. The hallway was dark and the door thick. I could hear Paul's voice behind it but not the words. So I pushed the door gently.

It gave. I put my fingers on Agnes' lips to keep her quiet and heard him say, "I'll simply have to, that's all. No, you call the sheriff. Tell him to get to my house quickly, that Peters is here threatening to kill me. When I hear the sheriff's car pull up, I'll shoot them and put a gun in Peters' hand, a gun with a bullet recently fired. No, I'll be careful. There's still too much more to do."

I closed the door and led Agnes back down the hall.

"That bastard is going to kill us," she said aloud. I clamped my hands over her mouth and shook my head negatively. I got her back in the living room, told her to lean back and pretend to sleep, and I sat rubbing my eyes.

Paul, massive and now deadly, came back in the room carrying a huge plierlike black steel tool.

"This should do it," he said. I held up my right hand and Agnes' to reveal the handcuffs. His story to the police about having to kill us would go better if we seemed less hopeless and he more vulnerable.

Agnes looked up at him with more hatred than fear, and I gave her a look designed to keep her from giving anything away. Paul fit the pliers over a steel link and pressed down with both hands. His body shook under his gray suit, and then the link snapped, and Agnes and I came apart. We each still had a bracelet, but the sense of regaining our own separateness was a nice shock.

"The police will be here shortly," he said. "I'll get you a drink. Bourbon, beer, coffee, tea?" he asked as amiably as his face, body, and probable madness would allow.

"I don't know about Agnes," I said, rising with a stretch, "but I could use a washroom."

"Me too," agreed Agnes.

Paul looked at his watch and figured, as I hoped he would, that there was plenty of time for us to get to the washroom and back before the police came. It was either that or pull out the gun now and hold us, which had other risks, including a pair of victims who weren't surprised and might cause some trouble at the very moment when they were supposed to be catching bullets between their teeth.

"Right down the hall near the kitchen," he said. "I'd suggest you hurry. The state police are not far off, and they said they'd get here quickly."

We thanked him and went into the hall. Next to the kitchen where we had overheard Paul's phone call was the partially open door of the bathroom.

"You first," I said to Agnes with a yawn and closed the door before she could step in. I looked back toward the living room, but Paul didn't step out. Agnes followed me into the kitchen. The door to the outside was bolted. I pushed the bolt back slowly, turned the latch and opened the door. It made a little noise.

"Peters?" came Paul's voice.

"Let's run like hell," I said and held her hand as we stumbled across the lawn. We had just reached the low wall when the first shot came. It chunked into the wall, sending a spray of yellowish fragments in front of my eyes. Agnes scrambled over the wall with me behind, followed by a second shot that whizzed across the road. We crouched behind the wall and did an ape scramble across the road. We could hear Paul coming after us, and I hoped he would guess wrong and try to head us off toward the beach. When we hit the small road in front of the house, I glanced back and saw Paul leveling a small rifle at us.

I pulled Agnes down, and the third shot caught a piece of the heel of my right shoe. The closest cover was some tall grass a dozen feet away, and he was sure to get a shot off before we were up and moving. I squeezed Agnes' hand, gave her my devil's grin, and began to roll into the road. She did the same. It seemed like a good idea, but it almost got us killed by the car that sped out of Paul's driveway and stopped inches from my head.

The car door opened, and an arm reached out to grab me and lift me like a teddy bear into the front seat. The arm went out again and pulled Agnes in as the fourth shot screamed through the car door and lodged in the seat near my shoulder.

"Jeremy," I said. He drove away as a fifth wild shot went over the car.

"I was watching the house, watching Paul," he explained, looking back in the rearview window. A car had stopped in front of Paul's house. It was a small car, getting smaller in the mirror, but it was clearly Alex and Nelson, who got out of it and met the massive Paul, who pointed in our direction.

"You see?" I said.

Jeremy nodded and stepped on the gas. The car was Shelly's Olds, and it proved to be reliable as always. Nelson and Alex might have caught us if they had had a little driving nerve, but that had probably been taken out of them earlier in the day by a snake and a crash. Neither of them wanted to risk nonsurvival in a second accident.

"Why not just leave me off at the side of the road?" said Agnes. "I like a little excitement, God knows, but this is going a little far."

"Sorry, Agnes," I explained, as Jeremy took a corner and sent me up against the door. "Paul knows we ran, knows we know he tried to kill us. If he spots you, he'll pull the trigger and claim you had a gun, or he went mad, or who knows. No, let's get back to the circus. I'm almost close enough to taste it."

"The killer?" asked Jeremy. "But isn't Paul the killer?"

"Nope," I said, leaning back to rest. "He's only half the tale."

"There is little poetry in the world," sighed Jeremy, turning another corner.

"We need what we can get," I said with eyes closed.

"I too thought that not long ago," he said. "But I no longer think it. This is a world of steamy woe, Toby. Poetry is necessary, yes, but for the poet, not the public. It took me this half a century on earth to understand that basic truth."

We hit a bump, and Agnes squealed in the back seat. "I think the nights are too cold in California," she whimpered, as the first chill of evening whistled through the bullet holes in the rear window.

"Yes," agreed Jeremy, "too cold for poetry."

"No," she sighed, "too cold for Abdul."

"You have a sick Arab brother, husband?" Jeremy said in sympathy.

"Snake," I explained. "Abdul's her snake. He got lost."

"We each fight our own wars," he said. "I have a snake poem which might comfort you. It's in the spring issue of *Southern Thought Magazine.*"

Agnes didn't pick up on the invitation. It was the least she could do for someone who had just saved her life, but then again, her life wouldn't have needed saving if I hadn't accused her of murder.

"I'd like to hear it, Jeremy," I said.

Agnes came out of her grief for Abdul enough to pick up on the signal I was giving her. Jeremy probably picked it up too. He had known me longer than she had, but he wanted to do it, and as he said, it was more for the poet anyway.

I opened my eyes and looked at him. There was a calm smile on his face as he performed.

> *What once were legs are no more*
> *in the cool perfection*
> *of form that seeks no complication*
> *and neither wishes to please or score.*
> *It kills without abuse,*
> *consumes without excuse,*
> *craves no company*
> *and keeps its counsel close to the earth.*
> *Hated for its distance and distaste*
> *for the image of standing man,*
> *the snake in his indifference becomes*
> *the symbol of the beast who can*
> *tempt us from the garden of ignorance*

by his very example
of independence.

"Some snakes kill very violently, and a lot of them like company," commented Agnes. "I mean, I like the poem . . ."

"It is not about the reality of snakes," explained Jeremy patiently. "It is about man's image of the creature, my image of the creature. The total number of subscribers to *Southern Thought Magazine* is no more than two hundred, and I doubt if any of the dozen or so who will read my poem are herpetologists. I don't care about snakes. It's metaphor I'm after."

"Well," said Agnes, "I don't care about metaphors or Seventh-Day Adventists. I care about snakes."

"A realist critic," sighed Jeremy, with a sudden turn down the road to the circus.

chapter 12

There wasn't much doubt that Paul, Alex, and Nelson would either follow us to the circus, lose us and head for the circus, or just realize where we were going.

The circus lights glowed yellow in the twilight over Aldreich Field, and we followed those lights like the North Star. Jeremy drove right to Emmett Kelly's wagon and parked the car behind it. I told Agnes to stay with me, but she said she was going back to her snakes.

"They're hungry and scared," she said.

"I'm sorry," I told her. "I mean, I'm sorry I thought you had anything to do with the murders."

She kissed my nose and ran off. I asked Jeremy to stay with her just in case Paul or anyone showed up who might be a problem. He nodded and went off after her.

Kelly, Gunther, and Shelly were inside the wagon, and all three leaped up when I stepped in.

"Are you all right?" said Gunther.

"Is Agnes all right?" said Kelly, dressed as Willie.

"My car," said Shelly. "Jeremy took my car."

"Agnes is fine. I'm fine. The car's outside with one neat bullet hole in it."

Shelly ran for the door and out.

"I've almost got it wrapped up," I said, "but I need a little more time."

"The clown suit," said Kelly, who was in his Willie costume. I winced and then agreed. Gunther hurried along at my side as we headed for clown alley, and I explained what I wanted him to do.

"There is probably a much simpler way than such direct confrontation," he said reasonably. He was always reasonable.

"Maybe," I said, winding my way through the crowds to keep an eye on Kelly, whom the people kept stopping to gawk at, "but I haven't got any real proof, just someone caught in a lie and my word and Agnes' against Paul's. This is his town. I don't even have a motive. I've got to turn over a killer before the killer turns me over."

"Us," corrected Gunther, running at my side.

"Us," I agreed, looking down at him.

"Be cautious, Toby," he warned. "Some day your recklessness . . ."

" . . . will save the world," I finished with a wink. Gunther walked away, shaking his head, and I followed Kelly into the tent, where the clowns were putting the finishing touches on their costumes.

"Help needed here," Kelly said. Three clowns, one with a mop of orange hair and a huge painted grin, hurried over. He had a pipe between his teeth. Two other clowns, one a midget, leaped to our side.

"We've got to get him back in paint and fast," explained Kelly. "Town cops are after him, and he's got the Tanucci killer coming down."

No one spoke. There were a few nods and some hands grabbed me, began to strip my clothes off. First the inner tube went around my waist. Then the costume went on over it. My face was covered with something sticky, and the little hat was on again with the rubber chin strap. Someone thrust the fake lasso in my hand, and hands stood me up. I looked in the mirror at my side and saw that Toby Peters was gone.

"Just stay behind me," said Kelly as Willie. "Spin the rope and I'll do my act. I'll look back at you every once in a while as if you're following me. When I look at you, you look out at the audience, very slow, as if you want me to think you're not following me, and keep twirling the rope. Got it?"

I said I did, and I followed him into the night. The band was playing in the big top, and the stragglers were buying up their tickets for the final night of the Rose and Elder circus in Mirador. Kelly, two clowns, and I ran right past Alex and Nelson, who were at the entrance with their hands touching the steel of holstered guns. A few dozen yards behind them was Paul, who stopped still when we passed and looked directly in my eyes. I tried not to return the look as I passed, but that split face was irresistible. He recognized me as surely as I recognized him. I half expected him to yell for Nelson, but he didn't, and as I ran into the big top, I knew he didn't want to risk confronting me before witnesses. I had to be done away with before I could talk.

The lights hit me, and I was aware of something I had never felt before: eyes, thousands of eyes looking at me from beyond the brightness. There was a cheer in my direction, our direction. I was a clown. I followed Kelly and watched as clowns drove around in little cars, carried pails of water which they threw at each other, hoisted ladders, and drew howls of laughter. Willie walked in front of me, doing his wood-sawing act and taking it right into the stands. The first time he looked back at me I twirled my lasso harder and looked up at the crowd the way he had told me to do, a Jack Benny look. The entire section of the stands, hundreds of them, laughed. They laughed at me. They laughed at me because I had done something funny. I knew Kelly had set up the laugh, but it was a feeling I had never had before, as good as anything I had ever felt except for sex, handball, and the moment of facing what you most fear.

We were walking around doing a counterpoint to the

music when I spotted Alex at the entrance on one end of the tent. Nelson stood at the entrance to the other end, scanning the crowd. I didn't see Paul or his partner, but I knew they couldn't be too far away.

"They're waiting for me," I whispered to Kelly. Willie turned slowly to look in both directions, took off his hat, rubbed his head to the delight of the crowd, and headed to the center ring while the other clowns exited.

"And now," said the ringmaster over a crackling loudspeaker, "we direct your attention to the center ring where the Flying Ibems of Peru will dazzle you with their death-defying feats of antigravity."

Kelly held the rope ladder at the bottom, and I dropped my lasso and held the other ladder. The Ibems came out, bowing to the crowd to the sound of music, and advanced on us.

Their smiles never left their faces, but as they climbed the ladder each one in turn mumbled something about our not getting into their act.

"Don't worry," Kelly said without moving his lips. "They'll get more response because we're here. They'll probably ask me to do it again in the next town. Just pretend you're afraid they're going to fall. Hold your hat on your head with one hand and run around under them. Keep an eye out for your friends to leave."

Everything worked the way Kelly wanted. The crowd went wild, and the Ibems were sent out with a wild ovation.

"Now the crowd thinks the Ibems are good sports," said Kelly. "Let's get out of here."

Willie moped ahead of me, and I followed, picking up my lasso and twirling it slowly. The crowd applauded us to the entrance, and Kelly exited with his head bent over.

A figure barred my way, appearing between Kelly and me, a big figure in a costume that looked like a clown's version of a ringmaster. He was dressed entirely in green, including a high green hat with a white feather. His face was painted with yellow greasepaint, and he held something long and metallic in his hand. Even behind the paint there was no problem recognizing the split-faced Paul, who pushed me back with his belly into the tent.

Another set of acts was coming in, but I couldn't see them. The lights had gone down and the music was softer. I was aware of twirling human figures and shadows above us as I backed into the tent.

"This," said Paul softly, holding the shaft in the air, "is an elephant prod. A good jolt from this can make any, even the largest elephant, rethink his rebellion. An extra-good jolt can be a definite danger to an elephant and can easily kill a human."

He thrust the metal rod at me, and I tumbled backward. My eyes met those of a thin woman in the front row.

"He's trying to kill me," I said.

The woman's cheeks puffed out, and she put a hand over her mouth to stop the laughter.

Paul played his part perfectly, thrusting out his stomach and walking as he pursued me. I scrambled to my feet and tried to run, but the damn inner tube kept me off balance. Paul advanced, holding the prod over his head and whirling it.

I tried to convince four or five men, women, and children that this was no act. I looked up at the glittering women swinging on ropes for help, but they were too far away. The prod hissed through the air and missed my face by inches.

"The circus did this to me," Paul said, pointing a thumb at his grotesque face.

"Let's talk," I tried.

He shook his head to let me know that he had no more to say on that subject. "I had forgotten what it sounded like to have the crowd," he said angrily. "You hear them? That murmur, attention. We'll give them something to murmur about."

The steel rod thrust at me like a sword, and a spit seared through my purple costume and singed the white puff of a button. Paul lunged forward, and the crackling rod punctured my inner tube, which popped and sent a little girl near me into tears.

Released from the tube, I turned and ran for the far exit. Paul was behind me, but I had less weight and more to lose. The crowd went wild as I passed, and high above, I could hear one of the swinging girls shout that I was ruining her act.

I darted through the tent flap, looking for Nelson now instead of trying to avoid him. Things weren't going quite the way I wanted them to.

I looked around for help, saw none, and headed for Elder's wagon or where I thought Elder's wagon was. It took me a few seconds to realize that I was going in the wrong direction. The hulking form of Thomas Paul was outlined behind me, elephant prod in hand, coming steadily. I ducked behind a tent, unsure of whether or not he had seen me, tried to get my bearings, and wondered how I could lure him back to Elder's office without getting killed. There seemed to be no sound of footsteps, so I decided to peek around the tent. The prod sizzled through the canvas and missed my nose by the thickness of a defense stamp. I could smell the heat.

I bounced off the tent, and a second thrust burned through the canvas where my head had been. The tent ripped, and Paul stepped through. Then the chase went on, and I lost track of where I was and wondered where Paul had picked up all that speed with all that weight. There was a wagon at my back and a dozen places Paul could leap out of. The wagon had a rung ladder. I climbed, trying to keep my baggy clown pants from getting in my way, and stood on top of the wagon. I spotted Paul, and he spotted me. He was on the ground a few dozen feet away. We looked at each other for a second or two, and I yelled for help as he came toward the wagon and up the ladder. The big top was only six or so feet away, and the band was playing a loud wild march that helped drown out my scream. Paul came up, with prod ahead of him, swinging. I leaped to the tent and turned to face him. He followed to the end of the wagon and came after me with an enormous leap that shook the huge tent. Below us, I could hear a few cries of surprise where he had landed.

I backed up, grabbing at canvas, and Paul came resolutely after me.

"Let's talk," I said, going higher and higher, feeling the night wind through my greasepaint. Yeah, I thought, let's talk, one crazy clown to another on the night of a full moon, thirty or forty feet up in the air on a piece of canvas.

"My sister died in the circus," he said, coming after me.

The people under the big top must have seen the billowing and wondered what hell demon or animal was leaping over them.

"My father, my brother, and my wife died in the circus. Only the two of us survived, and look what it did to me. My face and my brain. We fell. We fell. I remember my father dropping the balance pole and floating past me."

We were moving steadily upward to the top of the tent, and he obviously had a better sense of balance than I did.

"And," he said, "the circus just went on. That very next day, as if we had never existed. The show must go on. Why must the show go on? Why do those people have to watch near-death to enjoy their own lives? That world below us is a corrupt world."

He stood holding the canvas with one hand and pointing downward with his other. The prod was his pointer, and he was God, and there was no reasoning with God.

"I tried to forget," he said. "I didn't want any part of it. I knew what he had done to the elephants, but I wanted to forget. Then this circus had to come here, to Mirador, the first circus to come here. They followed me, brought their corruption right to the place where I had retreated. They declared war. He was right. He told me and I tried to hide, but they followed me."

He took a lunge toward me, and I moved up higher, but there wasn't much higher to move, and his confession was doing me no good up here with no one but me to hear it and no one to save me.

"So it was his idea," I said into the wind. A flag was flapping at the top of the tent, and I reached it and clung to it. A strong wind had come up. If I let go, I would probably slide down the tent and into the darkness below to hit the ground or something worse. The best act in the circus was going on where no one could see it.

Paul came puffing up after me. His green hat went flying with a gust of wind.

"Why kill me?" I said.

"Because you know who we are," he shouted into the wind. "Because someone must be labeled killer if we are not to be."

"They'll catch you," I said.

Paul laughed, a sincere Santa Claus laugh. "You don't understand. We don't care if they catch us as long as we destroy all this, make people realize what a sham this is, this thing that kills families for entertainment."

It was not the time to reason with him. I could have compared the circus to boxing, which I liked, or the war going on in all directions, which I didn't like.

"Let's . . ." I started, and he made a wild lunge toward me, prod out. It went past my neck, and I swung my right arm at Paul's face. My fist was weak and backhanded, but I had forgotten the severed handcuff that was still on my wrist. It hit him in the face. The prod dropped from his hand, seared through the top of the tent, and plunged down into the sudden light. I looked down to watch it bounce off the side of the ring and send a prancing white horse leaping in fear. I could see crowd faces looking up in our direction.

Paul wasn't ready to give up. It was clear to me that he planned never to give up. He dug his fingers into the canvas and came back at me. I kept one hand on the flag, which flapped in my face, and tried to ward him off with my manacled hand.

"You'll kill both of us," I said reasonably.

Paul was still not listening. He lumbered forward and clamped his arms around my waist. I pounded at his head with my handcuff. He squeezed and tried to pry me loose from my perch. His arms were powerful, and I could feel my head going light. It was no time to meet Koko, plunging into unconsciousness. I'd never come out of the inkwell this time. I pounded at

Paul's head and yellow face as if at a bent nail refusing to go into hard wood.

I was getting nowhere one-handed. It was time to do something. I let go of the flag and threw a left into Paul's neck. He groaned and let go for an instant. When he did, I kicked him in the chest and he tumbled backward, clutching at canvas. I grabbed the flagpole again as I felt myself starting to slide away.

Paul's right leg was through the hole he had burned in the top of the tent. He was dangling, grabbing for the tearing canvas. We locked wrists and hands, and I held on, feeling the tear in the tent widen with Paul's weight against it.

"You hear?" he said, dangling and looking up at me with that split yellow face. "They're enjoying it. They're waiting for us to fall so they can tell their aunts and sisters how they paid a few cents to see someone die."

"We'll disappoint them," I said, trying to pull Paul up but feeling his weight increase with each slight tear of canvas and the perspiration of both our hands.

"No, we won't," he said. "You'll never be able to pull me up. But I'll be able to pull you down. We'll give them a show. We'll land right in the center ring laughing at them, you and I, two clowns of hell."

He was right. My grip on the flag was giving way, and he was holding me in a death grip.

"Swing up," I said. "Swing up, damn you, you lunatic."

"Join me," he said, looking down at the stunned crowd below. He bounced up and down, laughing. The socket of my left arm went sore and numb, and I let go of the flag, but we didn't plunge through the hole. We slid forward, and Paul, convinced that I was following him into the bright air of the big top, let go of my hand. My leg hooked onto the rope holding the flag, and my head and shoulders went through the hole. I watched Paul, dressed all in green, spin over and over and land with a thud in the silence. It was all upside down and slow, and I felt sleepy. I hung for a second or two and realized that there was still silence, a silence of people expecting me to come plunging through the hole. I disappointed them, eased my way back up to the outside with my good hand, and sat for a long time clinging to the flag. The trip down was slow. My arm was sore, my back was sore again, and the chance of slipping in the wind great, but no one was chasing me with an elephant prod. I waved at the moon, and maybe he waved back.

I made it to the point where I had leaped from the wagon to the tent but didn't have it in me to make the leap back. I hung down by one good arm and dropped to the ground.

There was still a lot to do. No one had heard Paul confess. As far as Nelson was concerned, I was still a killer. He might have some trouble figuring out why Paul was dressed like that and what he was doing on top of the tent, but that wouldn't stop him. No, I had to give him a wrapped killer if I was going to get out of this, and luckily, there was still a killer left. Paul hadn't confirmed much, but he had confirmed something about the second killer. My only fear was that there might be three killers or four or five. How many members of Paul's family had survived that plunge from the high wire? I was pretty sure of one, but it was getting to the point where I would have to gather the suspects.

I slunk around the tents, moving away from the big top and the noise, toward someplace where I could rest for a few minutes before putting things together.

I could hear people running toward me in the darkness, and I spotted a familiar tent. I plunged into it. It was dark and warm. I could feel the animals rustling in their cages.

"I think he went in there," came a voice.

I ran behind the nearest cage, and the cat inside bellowed. In the entrance stood someone with a flashlight. The light beamed into corners, and I hovered behind the wheel of the wagon. The figure took a step into the tent and was stopped by the darkness and a loud animal snarl. The figure was small and looked to me like Nelson. The figure backed out.

"Not in there," he said, and I knew it was Nelson.

There was time to catch my breath. I sat on the cool ground, telling myself that it had really happened, that Paul had really plunged through that hole. I knew I'd see him in my dreams.

Something rustled outside a cage in the darkness.

"Who is it?" I said, getting to my feet. No answer.

My eyes were getting used to the dark, and I could see the green-yellow eyes of animals following me as I crouched and moved toward the rustling sound.

"I've got a gun," I lied. "Step out into the middle of the tent or I'll shoot."

No one stepped into the middle of the tent.

"Your gun is in the hands of the police," came a voice from the dark.

I wasn't sure where the voice came from, but I took a chance and leaped around the lion wagon, ready to throw a punch with my good remaining arm. There was no one there, but someone was suddenly behind me, someone who had moved quickly and hit me now with the weight of the world before my sore back would let me turn.

My skull is worn thin by nearly half a century of my using it to ward off attacks instead of as protection for my brain, which should have been thinking.

As the blue darkness with little stars skittered in my head like the beginning of life or time, a voice said, "For my brother."

Koko, the clown of my dreams, reached out for me, and I tried to pull my hand away. I have a brother too, I wanted to say. But Koko wanted to play, and there was, as I now knew, no turning down a determined clown. I took his hand and went into the inkwell.

chapter 13

And that is how I came to be encaged with a snoring gorilla.

My choices were now clear. I could stand perfectly still when he woke up and pretend I wasn't alive. I didn't know how long I could keep that up or how much I could expect a gorilla to believe. I could also simply go about my business, pretend that I frequently found myself in cages with bad-tempered apes and act as if I were washing out my clown costume or cleaning my nails on my knee. A third choice was to start jumping up and down and making as much noise as I could in the hope that Gargantua would be too surprised to act. Even if it worked, which was as far from likely as Herbert Hoover making a comeback, I didn't think I could keep it up.

Enter Henry. He came through the opening in the tent and looked directly at me. His finger went up and his mouth fell open. I tried to motion to the cage door, but Henry had other plans. He fell over on his face and lay there as if he had been laid out by Joe Louis.

He was either my killer's victim number three, the object of a heart attack, or dead drunk. I was giving myself a lot of options for a lot of things. I guess that's what you do when you lose control over a situation.

"Franklin D. Roosevelt," came the words from Henry. He was drunk. The words were said without Henry bothering to move his head. Gargantua stirred and scratched his right leg with his long fingers.

"Franklin D. Roosevelt said tonight," Henry went on, turning his head and starting to sit up, "that we were living in violin times. I don't understand. Who understands? Maybe he meant violent times. No. That is no better. I had that map of the world out, just like Franklin D. said. Franklin D. coughed a lot tonight. If he's getting sick, we are lost. 'Flying high and striking high,' he said. 'American eagle isn't going to imitate an ostrich or a turtle.' "

I considered whispering to Henry and even let out a controlled "Pssssssst."

But he wasn't buying any. He was too busy analyzing the President's latest fireside chat. His head swayed as he sat on the ground and tried to find Gargantua in the dark. "I think," he said emphatically, "that Franklin D. is a man of the people. Yes, a man of the people, but what have violins or violets got for Chrissake to do with it?"

"Violence," I whispered.

"Thank you," said Henry sincerely. He got off the ground slowly, using a nearby cage for support. "Violence," he mused. "Now that makes sense."

The issue settled, he turned his back and took one tentative step toward the outside. I had to risk it.

"Henry," I whispered. Nothing. "Henry," I whispered louder. Gargantua definitely stirred. Henry stopped and looked back at the cage.

"I am drunk," said Henry. "I ain't very much in the way of smart, but I know when I am drunk, for I am a drinking man. Gor-yellas don't talk. They can't. Can't even teach 'em."

"It's me," I said, almost breaking the whisper, "Peters, Toby Peters. I'm locked in the cage."

Uncertainty clouded Henry's brow. I could see it in the

half-light of the approaching dawn. He took a few steps toward the cage, and I expected him to fall on his face again.

"In the cage?" he asked.

"Get me out," I said, glancing at Gargantua, whose eyelids were fluttering. "Fast."

Henry walked to the cage a few feet from me and grabbed the bars to keep from falling over. "You are not supposed to be in there," he said with all the authority he could get together. "You are supposed to be out here."

In case I didn't know where "out here" might be, he pointed at it. "Out here" proved to be a few inches above the ground in front of him.

"Get me out of here," I whispered. Gargantua was definitely coming awake now. I tried not to move, but it was hard to watch both the gorilla and Henry without at least turning my head.

"I'm sure as hell getting you out of there," said Henry resolutely, without moving. "Out of there and over here."

Gargantua picked his nose dreamily and ran a finger down the side of the cage. He didn't seem to notice me.

"If you don't open the cage," I sang, near hysteria, "I'm going to get torn apart."

Henry considered this possibility for a moment by looking down at his feet. My impulse was reasonable and sane. I wanted to reach through the bars and kill Henry. Gargantua definitely looked in my direction.

"Henry," I said softly, smiling at the gorilla, "if you don't get me out of here now, please, I'll beat the hell out of you."

Henry laughed and shook his head. "Can't beat the hell out of anything if GooGoo tears you up."

He was right. Sometimes even drunken fools or private detectives are right.

"I'll curse you," I said as Gargantua stood and cocked his head to one side to be sure that what he thought he saw was actually in the cage with him.

"Curse?" asked Henry, lifting his head. I had his attention. "You mean like the evil eye?"

"Right," said I, turning my back to him to face Gargantua, who cocked his head to the other side. "I have the evil eye. Got it from my aunt. I'll give you a blast from it if you don't get me out of here."

Henry began to move. He pushed himself away from the bar and I lost sight of him, though I could hear him moving. I couldn't take my eyes off Gargantua, who took two steps toward me.

"Hurry," I said, not knowing whether Henry was opening the cage or running in drunken madness from my evil eye. A second or two later I knew he hadn't gone. I heard his voice.

"Goes around throwing people through tents and does who knows what else and then says he'll give me the evil eye," he mumbled. "Me, Henry Yew, who has almost never done bad . . . except maybe the time with my cousin Parmale."

Gargantua was now definitely interested in whoever was in his cage and was standing in front of me, looking down. I thought I heard other sounds, footsteps, maybe even words in the tent, but they couldn't get through to me. Nothing could get through to me but that dark face over mine, looking curious and benevolent. I thought I heard the cage door opening, but I couldn't move. I couldn't even think of moving. I couldn't even think when Gargantua decided to start pounding on his chest. It sounded like a half-empty oil drum echoing to eternity.

I nodded my head in appreciation at the skill and artistry of his chest pounding. He pranced around the cage a few times, still pounding his chest.

"Really nice," I said to him with an admiring and idiotic shake of my head. "Henry," I shouted and glanced at the door of the cage. It was definitely open. A voice beyond it whispered, "Come on." I slid a few inches toward it, and Gargantua stopped and roared.

"Just go on pounding," I said to him softly. "Go on."

But there was to be no going on. He showed his teeth and took a step toward me I didn't like. The door to the cage flew open and banged, metal against metal. Gargantua turned to the sound, and I crawled toward the door on hands and knees.

While a great warm hand grabbed at my slithering back, leaving a print which would probably stay for weeks, something else leaped into the cage. I tumbled through the cage door to the ground and turned to see Jeremy Butler facing Gargantua. The ape definitely looked puzzled. There had probably never been anyone in his cage before, and now he had a changing of the guard of mad humans. His hand went up slowly toward Jeremy while a low growl came from deep in his dark stomach.

Jeremy's right fist came up quickly, catching the gorilla in the nose and right eye. Gargantua staggered back in surprise. He was the one who was supposed to slap creatures around. Hadn't we read the posters?

In the instant it took him to recover and lunge for Jeremy, the former wrestler and present poet had dived out of the cage door. Several hands, not mine, pushed the door shut behind him, and Jeremy turned and rammed the lock shut. The cage shook as Gargantua battered the door in rage and bellowed in anger.

Gunther, Shelly, and Jeremy stood looking at me. Henry was seated on the rung of the two-bar ladder that led up to the cage.

"He liked you," said Henry toward my general direction. I had propped myself up against the nearby lion cage. "All that beating on the chest. Liked you. Or maybe he wanted to tear you up. Hard to tell with gor-yellas. Like people."

Gargantua was going on with the ferocity of one who has been cheated out of dessert or lost his high school sweetheart. I wasn't sure of how he viewed me. We hadn't had much time to talk.

"Toby," said Gunther, "the police are looking for you. We suggest you make a departure."

"We gotta get the hell out of here, Tobe," Shelly whined.

I looked at Jeremy, who nodded his head in agreement. Jeremy put an arm under mine and started me toward the door.

Behind us, Henry was getting the world confused even further.

"Franklin D. said something about gor-yellas and not getting into cages tonight," he mused. "Franklin D., every time he is on the radio says I am his friend. Friend to the President of the United States, Henry Yew."

We made it to the outside, and I stood on my feet, breathing in as much air as I could. "Thanks," I said.

"I wonder," said Jeremy in response, "if I could have downed him. He has strength but no real sense of leverage. Ultimately it would have been unfair. He made no contract with me to fight, and I had, in his eyes, invaded what little private space he has."

"You make him sound reasonable," I said. "Maybe you should be Secretary of State."

Jeremy's shoulders went up in a shrug.

We ambled forward with Gunther, for no reason I could see, in the lead. There were a few voices from wagons, some faint animal sounds, and us hurrying toward what I assumed was Shelly's car.

"I think I know who the killer is," I said.

"Perhaps," said Gunther, "but it will provide you no service if no one chooses to listen to you."

It was once again, as Gunther always was, reasonable. I had the vague idea that I would go somewhere, sleep, think for a few hours, and make Mirador and the Rose and Elder circus what they were before, while Franklin D. did the same with the rest of the world.

We made it to Kelly's. He was there and looking none too happy.

"Are you all right?" he said while I got out of what remained of my clown costume and into my last pair of trousers, a shirt, and my gray sweater with the brown reindeer on it.

"Let's go," urged Shelly.

"I'm fine," I told Kelly.

"Sorry I got you into this," he said, looking somewhat like Willie even without the makeup.

"It goes with the job," I said.

"I want you to get out of this," he said. "Just take care of yourself and send me a bill."

"I'll send you that bill," I said, "after I catch a killer. I'll be in touch." And out the door I went, followed by my faithful band of merry men from Los Angeles forest. "This handcuff has to come off," I said as we hurried in the general direction of Shelly's car.

"Easy enough," said the Sheriff of Nottingham, stepping out from behind a tent with a very large shotgun in his hands. We stopped. Behind us stepped Alex, also holding a shotgun.

"You shoot from there," I said, "and you'll kill each other."

"And you in the cross fire," said Nelson evenly, his white hat over his eyes.

"That hat doesn't make you a good guy," I said.

"Shut up, Toby," whispered Shelly. "Do what they say."

"I know who killed the Tanuccis," I went on with more confidence than I felt.

Alex took a step up behind us, and Nelson stood his ground.

"So do we," said Nelson. "Just put up your hands, all of you. You too, big fella and little fella, or maybe you won't have any hands to put up."

"I think," said Jeremy, lifting his hands and whispering to me, "we try to take them now. If they get you back to . . ."

"No," I said to him and then to Nelson, "OK. Let's go. You've got me."

"Indeed, indeed," said Nelson, rocking on his heels. "I have a whole menagerie, a regular conspiracy of freaks."

"You," said Gunther indignantly, stepping forward, "are a semiliterate dunderkopf."

"Sez you, peewee," Nelson answered. "All of you just move along slow and sweet, like the little girls at the Catholic school in Palm Hills, and we will be friends."

We moved in a single line with our hands up through the circus grounds and to a truck on the dirt road.

"Into the back of the truck," said Nelson. "I'm going to drive, and Alex is going to be in the car right behind. We are going to go very slowly, and if one of you happens to fall out of the truck on the way back, there is a very great chance of an accident involving you and Alex's car. We no longer have a police car. It met with a slight accident, the nature of which we will demonstrate on the person of Mr. Peters."

"You have a way with words, Nelson," I said, getting into the back of the truck.

Gunther had to suffer the indignity of being put up on the truck by Jeremy. Shelly needed the same help, but he didn't see it as indignity. He was too busy blaming me for his troubles.

"I'm sorry, Gunther," I said.

"You did not bring this to pass," said Gunther, trying to keep himself and his wardrobe clean as he stood holding onto a piece of rope. Jeremy made himself confortable and kept his eyes on Alex as we drove.

"I don't know how you talk me into these things," said Shelly, cleaning his glasses on his dirty jacket. "Mildred is not a fool. She told me something would happen if I came here. Mildred went to college like me. She had courses in things like philosophy. I should have listened to her. I'm a dentist."

I found nothing coherent in Shelly's rambling, so I tried not to listen.

"Do you really know who the killer is?" Gunther asked as we bounced around. It came out, "Do . . . uh, uh . . . you . . . uh, uh . . . really . . . uh, uh . . ." Hardly the conditions for a prolonged conference.

"I'm not sure. I'll tell you what I've got." And I told him. He listened, nodded his head, thought, and nodded some more.

"There is hatred in that face," Jeremy said, "but there is also something else too. Some sense of calm, balance."

"Who?" I asked.

"The deputy," Jeremy said, nodding to Alex in the car on the road behind us.

"He wants to kill me," I said.

"He is not the one to fear," said Jeremy. "It's the one in the front, the sheriff, a frightened man. He sweats too much and is too far away from what he really is. A frightened man who doesn't know who he is."

"I don't have to take that," shouted Shelly. "Being a land-lord doesn't give you . . ."

"He's talking about the sheriff," I explained, and from the front of the truck came Nelson's voice, "Shut up back there. We're in town, and I don't want you waking the dead or the citizens."

The truck came to a stop, and Alex parked right in the middle of the street. He came out of his car, shotgun in hand. Nelson came around to the rear of the truck with his weapon out.

"Now," he said. "You three and a half come out and get inside with no trouble."

As he got off first, Jeremy took a dangerous step toward the sheriff, who backed away and cocked his shotgun.

"It would be best," said Jeremy, "if you stopped trying to make something more of yourself by being offensive to us. It does not accomplish your end. In fact, it makes you look more pathetic."

We were all off the truck now, and I had the uneasy feeling that we might be gunned down where we stood. The Mirador Day Massacre. Nelson looked far from pleased. I glanced at Alex, who was looking at me, and tried to read his look, but there was no reading it.

We paraded into the Mirador police station, pausing for only a second to notice the boarded-up window Alex had destroyed the day before. The sun was up now, low but bright. It was going to be a sunny day and a long one, maybe a very long one.

chapter 14

"I'll have you laughing through a toothless mouth," hissed Nelson to Jeremy, as we prisoners sat on the small wooden bench while Alex turned on the lights.

" 'And if I laugh at any mortal thing, 'tis that I may not weep.' Lord Byron," said Jeremy.

"A bunch of smartasses," said Nelson between his teeth.

"Know your enemy and break his arm," said Jeremy, answering Nelson's look of hate.

"That is not poetry," said Gunther.

"In a sense," said Jeremy. "It was said to me before a tag-team match in 1937 by Strangler Lewis."

"I'm a dentist," announced Shelly, trying to get up. His glasses fell from his nose, and he managed to grab them blindly. He didn't see the two shotguns turn toward him.

"Sit down, Shel," I said, grabbing his arm. He sat down.

"A dentist, damn it," he repeated, putting his glasses back on and turning to me. There was a huge thumbprint in the middle of his left lens which Shelly ignored. "A few more years and I could have been a real doctor. Things like this shouldn't happen to people who could have been doctors."

"Now," said Nelson, putting his shotgun on his desk, which was about fifteen feet from where we sat. "Now." He got behind the desk, sat, and folded his hands. His white hat was still on his head, and the gun was within easy reach. Alex leaned back against the wall, shotgun up.

"You can be spared much discomfort," began Nelson, "if you simply tell me what happened, how you came to kill all these people, including one of the most prominent people in our town. You will do it slowly, and we will all go to bed. I have had a busy night and day and wish a few hours of sleep. In addition, I don't want to have to bring any state troopers back here. That would displease me."

"OK," I said. "We didn't kill anybody. Paul tried to kill me. He and a partner killed the Tanuccis and covered for it. Paul tried to kill me because I found out about it. I went to his house for help, and he tried to kill me and Agnes. Ask her."

Nelson's knuckles went white. "You mean the young lady with the snake? Your young lady from the circus? You know what her word is worth?"

"Compared to yours?" I said. "About two bucks for every nickel."

"Not funny, Peters," said Nelson.

"I have some bad moments," I admitted.

"Let us try again," said Nelson, removing his hat and placing it on the desk near his shotgun.

"Nothing to try. Paul hated the circus, used to be part of one, had an accident which messed up his face and mind and killed some of his family. He was nuts."

"That, I take it," said Nelson, "is your clinical opinion?"

"Then why the hell do you think he was dressed up like that, for climbing on top of the big tent? Was he your neighborhood eccentric? The town idiot?"

"Few towns have two official idiots," said Jeremy, looking at Nelson. I could swear I saw a smile in the corner of Alex's mouth. Nelson turned to him, but the smile was gone.

"I am a tired man," warned Nelson, fingering the shotgun, "and I demand civility."

"You earn civility," said Jeremy; "you do not get it by demanding it."

"Paul was out of his mind," I jumped in. "He came after me with an elephant prod, an electric thing, and I ran. He chased me up the tent and fell through. I tried to save him."

Nelson looked up to heaven for strength to tolerate such tales, but heaven didn't help him. "You are trying to tell me that a man would go around killing people . . ." he began.

"And elephants," added Gunther.

"And lions," added Shelly.

"No," I said. "The lion hurt his tooth . . ."

"Stop it," shouted Nelson, lifting his shotgun and banging the stock on the desk.

"Nelson, for God's sake, why the hell would I want to go around killing circus people?" I said, trying to sound as weary as I was.

"Hired," he said. "Someone had a grudge against those people and hired you down from Los Angeles to do some killing. You've been near some killing before. Right in this town."

"Sure," I agreed. "Killer for hire. Circus performers, animals. Someone just read my ad in *Dime Detective* and gave me an extra ten bucks to find an elaborate way to kill Paul."

"I don't need the why," insisted Nelson, who was obviously getting confused. "We caught you red-handed with one hand up your gee-gee and the other on the gun right on the beach."

"And what were you doing on the beach?"

"Mr. Paul called us and said he saw . . ." Nelson stopped.

"Something getting through to you, Nelson?" I said.

Everyone was quiet now. A clock on the wall, which had been ticking all the time, suddenly insisted on being heard. I listened to it.

"You haven't got a case against me," I said. "It wouldn't hold up long enough to make it worthwhile for my lawyer to come down here. He could probably handle it all with a phone call."

Nelson looked up at the clock. It was hanging over Alex's head and ticking for all it was worth. Nelson couldn't take his eyes off the clock for a hypnotized second or two, and then he forced them away.

"I've got a leading citizen killed here, a police car destroyed, a window in the police station beyond repair, a deputy attacked, two circus people murdered. I cannot walk away from that."

There was something definitely more reasonable in Nelson's voice. What little confidence he had in our collective or individual guilt was oozing through the floor, but he had to have something else. Nelson would rather turn us in than walk away dry without an answer. I'd seen it before when I was a cop. You nail somebody for a stickup or even a killing, and you hold tight even when you're sure he's not guilty. Hell, you even go to trial, knowing you're going to lose. Then when the judge or jury turns him loose, you shout fix and corruption and blame a weak system. Beats letting everyone know you have no idea who your killer is. That was the road we were going down now, and if I didn't get us off it, a killer would get away. Besides, I wasn't all that sure that a good prosecutor couldn't nail us with the killings.

"Do you want me to tell you what to do?" I said.

Nelson looked at Alex, who kept looking at us. "Talk away," said Nelson. "I can see no cost to listening."

"Right," I said. "I think I know who the killer is. . . ."

"You said you knew for sure," Nelson interrupted.

"I know for sure," I said, "but I've got no real evidence. If you work with me, I'll set the killer up for a confession you can hear."

It sounded reasonable even to me, but I had no idea how I was going to do it.

"What does this plan involve?" asked Nelson.

"You let me go, and I set it up. You keep my friends here to be sure I'm telling the truth."

"That is one rotten idea," shouted Shelly, starting to get

up, this time with a hand over his glasses. Alex motioned him back down, and back down he went.

"You know how much an extraction can really hurt if a dentist wants it to?" asked Shelly, looking at Alex with hatred.

"No deal, Peters," laughed Nelson, near the end of the nerve he was faking. "You'd walk out on this crew of misfits quicker than I could fall off the chair."

"No, he wouldn't," said Alex.

I had almost forgotten that Alex could talk.

Nelson turned his head to the deputy. "Well, well, an alienist in my own midst," snickered Nelson. "The man you are willing to believe is the man who made a fool out of you, deputy, a large Mexican fool."

"He wouldn't run," Alex repeated without emotion.

"All right," Nelson said with the trembling voice of hysteria and no sleep. "Supposing we agree to let you roam around while we baby-sit with your barrel of monkeys. What next?"

Gunther began to whisper furiously in my ear. It was a plan. It was simple.

"If he needs a bathroom, all he has to do is come out and say it," said Nelson. Gunther said it, and Nelson pointed the way. "No way out back there," he added.

"You want to hear the plan or not?" I tried, testing a slightly aggressive tone of my own as we watched Gunther move down the corridor between the cells. I gritted my teeth. I was taking over. Jeremy gave me an approving nudge. Shelly had his arms crossed and was looking at the boarded-up window, having dismissed us from his world.

"Go ahead," said Nelson.

He bought it. It wasn't an easy sale, and he reserved the right to demand his money back, but he bought it. It took a few minutes to work out the details, and the final one came only when Gunther returned and whispered something to me.

"I need the keys to the truck or the car," I said when I had finished.

"You want our shotguns too?" barked Nelson, but it was now the bark of a moody child.

"No," I said. "I'd like my gun back, but I can do without it if I have to."

"You have to," said Nelson. I knew he would. I just thought it better to give him something to save his face.

"Be careful, Toby," said Jeremy as Nelson handed me the key to the truck.

"I must be crazy myself," mumbled the sheriff.

There were no shock absorbers worthy of being called shock absorbers on the truck. I bounced without event down the street, which was just waking up. The door of Hijo's opened next to the sheriff's office, and someone was fiddling with the lock of the "Fresh Bate" store.

There was clearly no day of mourning for Thomas Paul of Mirador. I got to Paul's house after making a few mistakes, but I figured it out. It looked as if no one was there, and there might not be, but I had the feeling that there was. Gunther had said it was logical. Whoever was working with Paul would have to go back to his house to see if there was anything that could link the two of them. The killer might do it quickly or might take a long time. The killer might even say the hell with the whole thing and run for Acapulco.

But this killer had been in the game for a long time, had poisoned some elephants and started a fire the year before, had shared a hatred for the circus, and, if I was right, done some very dangerous and equally dumb things.

I parked in the driveway and went in, making a lot of noise. I didn't want to catch the killer there and get myself killed. I was after a confession where others could hear it. I went into the living room, kicking things, singing "Flat Foot Floogie" and alerting any living thing within a hundred yards. The person I was trying to alert was not a hundred yards away but upstairs somewhere. I heard the creak and the step, and then it stopped. I kept singing and hurried for the phone.

There was no click on the line to indicate that anyone had

picked up an extension. I asked for a number from the operator. It was 5454 and meant nothing to me.

"*Quién es?*" came a young man's voice.

"Right," I said loudly. "I'm out at Paul's place now."

"*Qué?*"

"No, no point in staying here," I said. "Look, it doesn't mean anything unless you're willing to tell the sheriff. Are you willing to tell him or not?"

"*Qué pasa aquí? Está usted, Manuel?*"

"I can't force you to do anything," I said with exasperation. "You can just pack up with the circus and go. Just forget two murders. If you saw who took the Tanuccis' harness, and it wasn't Paul, then it was someone working with Paul."

"*Es un chiste muy estúpido, Manuel.*"

"OK, then we talk. Come to town. Mirador. Right in the center of town there's a little bar called Hijo's. I'll be there in ten minutes. It shouldn't take you more than fifteen or twenty. We'll talk, and if you agree, we go to the sheriff. Look, they're trying to nail all this on me."

"*Loco en cabeza.*" He hung up, and I kept talking.

"Just come," I insisted. "Your life isn't worth a box of popcorn if the bastard knows what you saw."

I hung up the phone. I wondered whether I would have fallen for it, but it was hard to tell. I wasn't a killer and I wasn't crazy. Something creaked very slightly upstairs. I didn't want to give the killer a chance to consider getting rid of me on the spot. I counted on the killer wanting me to point out the possible witness at Hijo's, but I have been wrong so many times that I more than half expected a sharp phutt of a bullet hitting my back or the vibration of a chair against my head. I got neither. As I climbed into the cabin of the truck, I noticed a curtain move on the second floor of Paul's house. I drove on down the road.

The trip back was faster than the trip out. I knew my way now. I parked on the street in front of Alex's car, where the truck had been before, and stepped out. A little Mexican kid about nine stood outside the door.

"I seen you before," the kid said, squinting up at my bristly chin and unforgettable face. "You came through when that guy got bumped off. Hey, you the guy they was looking for last night who cut off old Two-face's head?"

"I didn't cut off anyone's head," I said. "Now beat it."

"Cost you," he said.

I looked at the sun, the white clouds, and then at the sweet-faced kid asking for hush money.

"What's the going price for covering a murder?" I said, digging into my pocket. I didn't want to keep talking, but I didn't want him messing the setup. I was willingly contributing to the delinquency of a minor.

"Four bits," he said.

"Reasonable," I said, giving him two quarters.

He took them in his hand and examined them carefully.

"You think I'm a counterfeiter in addition to a murderer?"

"Just being careful," he said, pocketing the coins. "Don't worry. I didn't see nothin', I don't know nothin', and I don't say nothin'."

I hadn't seen a car at Paul's house, but the killer wouldn't have been dumb enough to park in the driveway. It would take a few minutes to get to wherever the car was, but that car couldn't be far behind me now.

"Take it easy," I said to the kid, moving toward Hijo's.

"Hey, I take it any way it comes," he said with a big grin.

"Ever thought of being a movie producer?" I said in front of Hijo's.

"What's it pay?"

"Almost as good as hush money," I said.

"I'll think about it," he said seriously. "Hey, you're not going into Hijo's, are you? You can get in trouble in there, my old man says."

"Got to," I said with a grin. "I've got a killer to catch."

The kid looked at me like I was crazy as I pushed open the door and left the day behind me.

chapter 15

None of the boys were whooping it up at Hijo's saloon. I stepped back two days in time. There were three people at the bar, a drunk at a table, and music playing. They were the same three people I had met there the last time. Only the music was different. At least I think it was different. It was a woman almost weeping in Spanish.

The Falstaff Beer sign sputtered on the wall, trying to keep up with the weeping woman on the radio, but was a beat or two behind.

My eyes adjusted slowly to the bartender sitting behind the bar with his head in but one hand this time and what looked like the same cigarette drooping from his chubby lips.

"You still with the circus?" called Jean Alvero, the whore with the heart of a dove.

I stepped to the bar, eyeing Alex's brother Lope, who wore the same denims but might have changed his shirt. The only thing different about him was the bandage over his head and right eye.

"Right," I said, keeping an eye on Lope, who walked over to me. The drunk at the table was awake. It was early. He probably didn't pass out till nine or ten in the morning.

"No trouble," I said to Lope, holding out my hand. His smaller friend was standing behind him, thumbs hooked in his belt.

"No trouble," said Lope. "I was drunk the other time. I deserved this." He pointed to his head. "I'll buy you a beer."

"I'll take a Pepsi, and thanks," I said with my smashed-face grin, "but I don't think it will be healthy to drink with me."

Lope's remaining eye went narrow. He had put out his hand in friendship, and if I turned it away he was going to lose what was left of his face.

"Don't get me wrong," I added quickly. "I'm expecting trouble through that door, and I don't want anyone too near me when it comes."

Lope understood that. His eye opened wider. "I'm not afraid of a little trouble," he said, looking back at his faithful companion Carlos, who grinned broadly.

"Fair enough," I said. "Keep an eye on me from the end of the bar, and if trouble breaks out, go for the one with the gun, knife, or chair in his hand, providing it isn't me."

Lope grinned, I think, and belched something at the bartender, who tore himself away from the radio to get me a warm Pepsi.

Lope and Carlos returned to Jean Alvero. I toasted her with warm Pepsi. "I thought you come back to see Jean Alvero," she said. I'd noticed that opera and movie stars and whores referred to themselves in the third person. Maybe they had something in common.

"I did," I said, trying to watch the door without insulting my hosts by turning my back. "It was your beauty that drew me irresistibly to Hijo's, though my duty lay elsewhere."

"You full of crapola, gringo," she grinned.

And warm Pepsi and a jigger of fear. My killer was probably not exactly sane. I wondered if one could be inexactly sane.

The drunk at the table eyed me through two tiny holes of red, and the weeping woman on the radio stopped. For a beat or two of the heart all that could be heard in that dim bar was the sputtering of the Falstaff Beer sign. Then the radio burst forth with rapid-fire Spanish.

The door to the bar swung open, and I tried to keep from looking, but you can't ignore a crowd, and a crowd it was.

"There you are," came a voice, which was clearly Emmett Kelly's and clearly concerned. Behind Kelly came Elder, Agnes Sudds, Peg, Henry Yew, Doc Ogle, and assorted people I didn't recognize.

The drunk at the table sat up, perplexed, and the bartender turned the radio down, ready to cater the party.

Elder, Kelly, Agnes, and Peg detached themselves from the group and moved over to me. This wasn't what I wanted, planned, or expected. Hell, few things were what I wanted, planned, or expected.

"What are you doing out of jail?" asked Peg. "We went next door and that sheriff said you weren't there and slammed the door on us."

"What's going on?" asked Elder. Kelly looked puzzled, and Agnes smiled at me with something that I might have thought pert if she weren't wearing a hat, a little blue thing big enough to hide a snake or two.

"I can't explain," I said. "I just need a few minutes to be alone, to think. Have a seat, take a table. Drinks are on me. See what the boys in the back room will have. Whatever. Just give me a few minutes."

"What the hell is wrong with you?" demanded Elder.

Kelly turned his head slightly and our eyes met. I had the feeling he was sensing my thoughts. "Let's leave Toby alone," he said, touching Elder's arm.

"Toby," said Peg softly, "are you all right?"

I looked at the door and looked at Peg. Her hair was dark and down, and I realized that she reminded me of Ann, my wife, I mean Ann, my ex-wife, who was due to marry an airline exec who looked like a tall Claude Rains.

"Please," I said, turning my back and picking up the Pepsi.

"You bastard," hissed Elder behind me. "We came here to help you, and . . ."

"Come on," urged Kelly. "Let's sit down."

They moved away behind me, but I didn't turn back. The bar was now bustling with circus people ordering early-morning tequila, beer, and Squirt—a party. The bartender shuffled, the music blared, and I looked into the dirty dark mirror behind the bar to see figures shifting. I thought I could see the door. I looked at my glass of almost finished Pepsi. There was something at the bottom of the glass, probably my nerve. I held up the empty to Lope and shouted to the bartender to buy drinks for my good friends at the end of the bar.

"I want to confess."

The words came over the bustling sounds in the room. Conversation was cut in half, and then the voice repeated, "I want to confess."

All conversation stopped. The radio kept going, this time playing a guitar solo. I looked toward the voice in the middle of the bar.

Henry Yew, the animal keeper, was looking somberly at his amber glass of liquid. "A confession," he said, holding up the glass as if he were toasting the happy crowd. "I am guilty. I am not Henry Yew. I am," he said dramatically with a drunk's satisfied smile, "Henry Ackerman."

"So?" said Jean Alvero.

"So," repeated Henry, turning to the bar and his drink, squeezing between a pair of burly roustabouts, "I confessed."

"And . . ." asked Jean.

"And nothing," said Henry. "Nothing. That's it, my real enumeration."

"That's not interesting," said Lope.

"I knew a one-eyed dog trainer once," said Henry, looking at Lope.

Lope cocked his head like a bird so that he could see Henry with his good eye, and Henry mocked him by doing the same.

"I think maybe I'll take your skinny eye out," said Lope.

"He's just drunk," said one of the roustabouts, turning to face Lope.

"Hell," said Lope reasonably, "people in bars are drunk all

the time. That don't mean they have to be stupid."

"Who are you calling stupid?" said the roustabout.

"Stupid people like . . ."

"Drinks on me," I shouted, hoisting my empty glass and hoping the bartender wouldn't give me a refill. The crowd at the bar shouted their orders. In the dark mirror I could see Kelly and group watching my back and wondering what the hell was wrong with me.

It was possible my killer wouldn't come over to me, wouldn't make contact, that I'd stand at that bar for the next year or two, waiting for the war to end or armed Japanese soldiers to walk through the door, order a bottle of Black and White, and mow us down. But it didn't happen that way. The door to Hijo's opened, and a familiar figure walked in. My back was turned, but I saw the figure pause in the mirror, look around, spot me, and move in my direction.

I played with my glass, tried to realign whatever small dark things were at the bottom. Maybe I'd be able to read my fortune.

"Good morning," the killer said.

"Good morning," I answered without looking up. "What's your pleasure?"

"If the glasses are reasonably clean, a gin and tonic."

"The glasses are not reasonably clean," I said, showing my glass.

"Then," sighed the killer, "I'll do without it. It is a bit early in the morning."

"Right," I said. Emmett Kelly had stood up. I could see him in the mirror, could see that he was going to come to me. I shook my head no. Kelly paused and then sat down.

"I see," said the killer, leaning against the bar and squinting into the mirror. We were shoulder to shoulder, could have been taken for buddies. "I take it that our clown friend is the one you were to meet here. It was not a question," said the killer, "but an observation. I was aware that the charade at my brother's house was for my benefit. I have been around performers most of my life. I can spot a poor performance with no difficulty. Yours was not exactly terrible. It had some energy, but far from professional."

Jean Alvero's laugh broke through the other sounds. I turned to look at her. She was talking down the bar to one of the roustabouts. One-eyed Lope didn't look too happy about the social possibilities.

"Then why did you come?" I said.

My killer shrugged. The bartender moved to us behind the bar, removed his cigarette and opened his mouth to let us know he was taking orders.

"A beer," said the killer. "No glass, just bring the bottle."

The bartender moved away.

"Good idea," I said. "No contamination. Not that you should worry about contamination."

"Are you going to insult me?" asked the killer with an amused smile.

"I don't know," I said. "There was a full moon last night, and someone tried to kill me."

"That was me. You are remarkably heavy for your size. You are also remarkably durable. But perhaps we can remedy that."

The bartender returned with the bottle of Gobel beer. It was open, and my friendly neighborhood lunatic took a deep drink.

"Warm."

"House rules," I said.

"I don't really mind," came the answer. "I grew accustomed to warm beer when I was in England. The taste comes through. Now, if you will just tell me who you are to meet."

I turned around and put my arms on the bar the way Walter Huston had done in *The Virginian*. "Why should I tell you?" I said, looking at Kelly. The others had their heads together talking.

"Because I can simply pull the trigger on the gun I am holding under the eave of this bar and make a very large hole in your side."

"And then you'd be caught," I said reasonably.

"Yes, but if you don't tell me, I'll be caught anyway. This way I might be able to make an escape. I think I am being clear and logical."

"La Paloma" burst out of the radio. It sounded like the same group that had sung it the first time I entered Hijo's. Jean Alvero joined in, in a rather nice cracking soprano.

"You had me fooled," I said with a shake of my head. "You really did, but how long did you think you could carry it off?"

I turned to look my killer full in the face now, and he looked back at me, putting down his empty bottle of beer. Something approaching a smile touched his face.

"Who would peg Alfred Hitchock as a murderer?" he said, showing me the gun beside his medicine ball of a stomach.

"You are one bedbug," I said. "I saw a picture of the real Hitchcock in a movie magazine in a railroad station yesterday. Anyone could have spotted you at any time."

The man I had known as Alfred Hitchcock hunched his shoulders up. "It was a risk worth taking," he said. "If worse came to worse, and it has, it really has, I planned to confess that I was a circus buff and that I merely used Hitchcock's name because of my resemblance to him to gain access to the grounds."

An argument had started at the end of the bar. Lope and Carlos were part of it. Some of it was in Spanish. I had the feeling it was a debate over who was going to listen to the radio and who was going to listen to Jean Alvero.

"There isn't any witness," I said, turning away from the killer. "That was just to bring you out in the open."

"I thought it might be," he sighed, "but I couldn't take a chance. Besides, all is not lost. You are responsible for my brother's death. I'm the last of the family."

"And he went like the others," I said, picking at my teeth

with a fingernail. "Mind telling me your name? I can't keep calling you Mr. Hitchcock."

"Marish," he said, bowing slightly. "Miles Marish. My family were the Flying Marishes."

He paused as if I was supposed to know who the Flying Marishes were.

"The Flying Marishes," I repeated.

Down the bar, the bartender had intervened in the discussion by turning off the radio.

"The circus killed my family," he said. "My father and sister fell from the wire in 1937. My brother was disfigured, and I was trampled by an elephant. Under these trousers is a disfigured leg.

"I wanted only to destroy the elephants, all the elephants," he said. "The people were Thomas' idea. There were no killings until the circus came to Mirador, where he had been living. It was I who had followed circuses, destroying and describing it to him. The circus is . . ."

"I know," I interrupted, "he told me before he took his leap."

"You are not a sympathetic man," said Marish, all trace of English accent now gone.

"Some innocent people have been killed," I answered. "They have my sympathy, along with their families."

"The aerialist saw me electrocute the elephant. We had to do something. Then the woman . . ."

"Rennata Tanucci," I supplied.

"She followed me to Thomas' and threatened to have that elephant go wild. I hate elephants. She forced us . . ."

Shoving and the tense ramble of voices came from the end of the bar. The battle was about to begin. The circus had invaded Lope's retreat, and his honor demanded satisfaction. Elder moved from his table to try to restore order.

"Do we have anything further to discuss?" said Marish evenly.

"One or two more things," I said. "Can we retire to my

office?" I pointed to the back of the saloon, where a painted green light indicated a toilet.

Marish nodded, put his gun in his pocket, and followed me toward the back. We had gone about five feet when Emmett Kelly stepped in front of me.

"Toby, you look . . ."

"I'm fine," I said. "Just someone I ate."

I pushed past him, and he eyed Marish, who gave him his Hitchcock grin. We moved past Elder, who was holding back his roustabout with one hand and talking furiously with Lope. Elder was speaking Spanish rapidly and comfortably. It seemed to calm Lope of the single eye. But I wasn't calm as I pushed open the door under the green light and stepped in with Marish behind me. He locked the door and faced me.

There wasn't much room, just a toilet, some toilet paper hung by wire from the wall, a small basin with a dripping faucet and a dirty brown sink. The small mirror over the sink looked as if someone had soaped it for Halloween and no one had bothered to clean it. A newspaper was on the floor. I caught part of the headline and realized that the British were either winning or losing in Burma.

"It was most cooperative of you to come back here," said Marish pleasantly. Then his voice turned harsh. "I am most distressed about what you did to my brother."

"Your brother?" I asked, sitting on the sink. He backed away from me with the small gun out and sat on the closed toilet. My brother and I had once had a similar talk when he was about seventeen and I was fourteen. My older brother had given me some advice then, and I had made a wise comment. The result was a five-inch cut on my head. I had more to lose this time.

"Charles Marish, whom you sent to his death last night," said Marish angrily.

"But he was a killer," I answered, folding my arms.

"We have been over that," he said. "I told you why he and I killed those people. You clearly have no sympathy or understanding. You clearly don't understand the shallow corruption the circus represents, the squalid lives, the cheapness. The world would be better off without circuses."

"And you're personally going to destroy them all?"

"I would that it were possible," he said. "But I will have to be content to carry on for my brother and do what little I can. Now . . ." He held up the pistol.

"Did you try to kill Emmett Kelly, or was that your brother?" I asked.

"One of our few failures," he sighed, reminding me of the man he had impersonated.

"Why Hitchcock?" I asked quickly.

"I became an actor after the elephant accident," he explained. "I worked in England as an extra on *Jamaica Inn*. A few people actually mistook me for Hitchcock on occasion. In fact, I doubled for Charles Laughton on the film. I'm afraid I shall now have to kill you."

"Afraid?" I pushed away from the sink. The rear of my pants was wet.

"I will enjoy it," he said.

"I think I'll just have to deprive you of that pleasure," I said.

He shook his head. I looked into the corner over that shaking head and fixed on the transom. Curiosity took him, but he didn't turn.

"I'm looking at a shotgun," I said. "Through the transom. Sheriff's been listening to all this. His office is right next door. This toilet and the sheriff's share a transom. Flush the toilet in there, Sheriff."

A toilet flushed almost instantly, and Marish looked up at the transom. I went for his gun as he glanced up, and hell broke loose. I slammed his hand away and the bullet hit the wall, followed by an explosion and the shattering of the mirror as I banged into the wall below the transom. Shards of glass flew, and I covered my head.

"You crazy bastard," I shouted at Nelson, sinking to the floor and moving my arm away from my eyes. I could see that my pants were torn by the flying glass, but I was doing fine compared to Marish, who had a deep gash on his cheek from the shotgun blast. He was looking around for something with madness in his eyes. He panted the frightened pant of a fat man. I helped him look. We were probably looking for his gun, and I wanted to find it first.

"Don't move in there," came Nelson's voice. "Or I'll fire the second barrel."

"Nelson, no!" I yelled, spotting the gun and going for it. Marish let out a gasp and went through the door. I got to my feet, picking up a cut on my palm. I staggered out of the destroyed toilet and looked down the bar. Everyone was looking at Marish and me. Some had their mouths open. All had heard the explosion, and no one could miss the two shredded humans who had come through the door.

"Stop him," I shouted after Marish who was almost at the front door. He was leaving a trail of blood. No trail was needed, but my own knees weren't doing well enough to carry me forward.

Marish put one hand on the door. Behind me from the toilet I could hear Nelson's voice yelling, "What the hell is going on in there?"

The radio was now giving a calm male message in slow Spanish that made it clear radios were unaware of human activity. I didn't know if Marish would get away or where he would go. I didn't have to find out.

Emmett Kelly moved to the door and put a hand on Marish's shoulder.

"Hold it," he said. Marish turned, his wild bloody face showing all his hatred for the circus. The look took Kelly by surprise. He was used to a lot, but not that look of hatred.

Marish couldn't resist. He threw a wild fat right at Kelly, who ducked and came back with a push to Marish's chest. The fat man tumbled back over the Hijo drunk and went down in a lump.

I limped forward as Alex and Nelson came through the front door of Hijo's with shotguns ready.

People began to scramble for corners and scream.

"Hold it," I yelled. "Don't shoot."

Nelson's eyes were wild and frightened, but they were probably no different from those of anyone else in the room, except he had the shotgun.

"It's over, Sheriff," said Alex evenly.

Nelson looked over at Marish and aimed his barrel at the fallen form. "Right," said Nelson. "It's over."

It was at that point that my knees said the hell with it, and I crumpled to the floor, hoping for an inkwell.

When I opened my eyes after dreaming that Koko and I could fly over Cincinnati, I found the face of Doc Ogle.

"Full of holes," came a voice behind him.

"Me?" I asked with a croak, trying to sit up.

"You and the whole damn story," came Nelson's voice. I looked past Doc Ogle, who had trouble straightening up. Nelson and Alex were there. I was back in the sheriff's office on the bench.

"This man could use a hospital," said the doc, packing something in his black bag. "Lacerations, concussion, goddamn crazy handprint on his back."

In the cell beyond the first, I could see Marish, sitting with his head down. He turned his face toward me, and I didn't like what I saw. The stitches didn't bother me, but that look did. I turned away.

"I will explain it another time for you," came Gunther's voice. I turned my head in the other direction and saw Gunther, Jeremy, and Shelly.

"Don't bother," sighed Nelson. "I've got enough. I heard enough. Alex and I heard enough."

"You'll be a hero, Nelson," I said, sitting up. "Caught a killer single-handed in a bloody gun battle. May even make the San Diego papers."

"May at that," said Nelson, pursing his lips.

"We'll be happy to stay around and tell our part of this," I volunteered. Jeremy walked over to me and gave me an arm. Hell, he picked me up.

"That won't be necessary," said Nelson, clearly preferring

his own tale of his gun battle and whatever fantasy of heroism he was working on. "Just you and your friends pack up and get out. We don't need you in Mirador, and we don't need the damn circus either."

"We're going," I said. Shelly led the way out, and Jeremy supported me.

"Maybe we'll see you again sometime," said Alex, leaning against the wall.

I tried to read through his words and couldn't.

"Maybe," said the Spirit of Seventy Wounds, and off we went into the afternoon, closing the door of the Mirador police station behind us.

The circus people were leaning against or loitering near half a dozen cars and trucks in what looked like a vigil. Peg and Elder spotted me first and moved in my direction. The Tanuccis were with them, and Emmett Kelly stood to the side with Agnes Sudds.

"Are you all right?" said Peg.

"Terrific," I said.

"You look awful."

"Maybe I don't feel so terrific," I admitted. "In fact, I think I'd just like to close my eyes and wake up in my bed back in Hollywood."

"Alone?" came Agnes' voice from behind.

"I'll be happy to wake up," I said, feeling something dark come over me.

Emmett Kelly took a step toward me with his hand out and his mouth open. That was my last memory of him, silent and looking a little sad.

I was aware of movement, I think, and Shelly's voice talking about saberteeth. I was aware of snakes of green and Saint Patrick with an electric staff. I was aware of a body full of aches and the memory of a look of hate. And then I was aware of nothing.

The next time I woke up, I was just where I wanted to be, lying in my own room in Mrs. Plaut's boardinghouse on Heliotrope in Hollywood. My bed was there, the sofa with doilies I wasn't allowed to touch, and my wooden table and small refrigerator. I wanted to get up and have a bowl of Wheaties, but a hand reached out and pushed me back. It was a small hand. "You must rest without disturbance," said Gunther. We were the only two in the room. "The doctor has come here to look at you and declared you recoverable. The suggestion came that you be moved to a hospital, but I thought you would prefer . . ."

"I would prefer," I said, sitting up. I was under one of Mrs. Plaut's homemade quilts, dressed in a T-shirt and underwear and feeling an overall ache that made a lie of aches.

"A thousand natural shocks," said Gunther sympathetically, watching me sit up.

"Something like that," I said.

"It is that which flesh is heir to, Toby," he said, handing me a cup of tea he retrieved from the table. "It is a bit cool but perhaps better for you for that."

While I drank, Mrs. Plaut burst in. Mrs. Plaut was not a knocker. Even if she knocked, she would never hear the responding "Come in" or "Stay out," and there were no locks on the doors of Mrs. Plaut's rooms.

"Mr. Peters," she said, crossing her thin arms. She was a tiny pink woman somewhere between seventy-five and a thousand, with the strength of a determined terrier. "You haven't been killing people again, have you?"

"Not intentionally," I said, sipping tea. "And not on the premises."

"No more bodies here," she said, stepping in to straighten a chair.

"I promised," I said.

Satisfied, she dropped a bundle of handwritten sheets on my table. "Chapters," she announced. "Papa and the well and Uncle Damper's Eskimo wife."

Mrs. Plaut was under the impression that I was, alternately, an exterminator and a screenwriter. I had never been able to determine how she came to this conclusion or when she made the transition from one to the other. I think she didn't much care as long as I continued to make corrections of her family history, which was now well over 3,000 pages long. I was in for a night with Uncle Damper's Eskimo wife.

Mrs. Plaut exited, and Gunther took my cup when I finished.

"There was something different about this one, Gunther," I said. "I can't grab it."

"The circus," said Gunther, cleaning my cup in the small sink on the far side of the room. "It has traditionally been a source of amusement for the young, a hint of danger, but when one penetrates its . . ." He searched for an English word and couldn't find the right one.

"Whatever," I said and put my head back for a few days of rest.

Koko wanted to play. I told him to go away. I had had enough of clowns and dreams.

chapter 17

It was a Tuesday when I walked into the Farraday Building on Hoover Street, which housed the offices of those on the way in and out of society I counted among my acquaintances, including me and Shelly Minck.

I loved the smell of Lysol that greeted me. It told me the world was normal, that Jeremy Butler was back in his building cleaning and battling decay and the trespassing bums who could make their way into the building through any crack or hole open to them.

It was great to feel the eroded marble under my feet. I was home, weak but home. I got on the elevator, knowing it might take me anywhere from five minutes to a week to get to my office on the fourth floor. The elevator and I split the difference.

Shelly was working on a patient I hadn't seen before when I came through the door to our offices. He didn't hear me. Neither did the bum in the chair.

"The clown, you know, Emmett Kelly," Shelly was saying over the buzz of his drill. "I saved his jaw, his whole jaw. They called me down to work on him. And you know why?"

The guy in the chair grunted.

"Reputation," said Shelly, holding his cigar aloft. "You have a reputation, and the world will come to you."

The guy grunted in enthusiastic agreement. People in Shelly's chair generally agreed with anything he said.

"Shel," I said. He turned quickly, revealing his recently cleaned smock, and almost tore his patient's eyebrow off with the buzzing drill. Shelly's cigar went back in his mouth. "My car. Gunther said you took my car."

"Arnie's got it," he explained. "You can pick it up anytime. You want to see a rotten mouth?" He pointed at his new patient, who gave a sickly grin. The mouth was certainly rotten.

"I'm fine, Shel," I said, moving to the door of my own office beyond his.

"How are you, Toby?" Shelly asked, turning back to his patient.

I went into my office, smelled the dust, looked at the picture on the wall of me, my old man, and my brother with our dog, Kaiser Wilhelm. My private investigator's license was next to it, needing dusting, and the cracks in the wall were just where they had always been and belonged.

I grabbed my Little Orphan Annie Ovaltine mug from my desk, ignored the ring inside it, and stepped back into Shelly's office to get a cup of the darkness he made each day.

Shelly was humming "Perfidia," and the world was back in order.

In my office, I made out a bill to Emmett Kelly. I was fair. I'm always fair. I didn't charge him for clothing beyond my windbreaker and two pairs of pants. I didn't overcharge him for what Arnie the no-neck mechanic would make me pay for whatever damage my car had taken from elephants and bullets. When I had finished, the total came to $186. It seemed like not very much for the four-day lifetime I had put into the case.

I put the bill in an envelope and mailed it to the address Kelly had given me. Then I sat back to enjoy my aches and Ovaltine. There was some mail, but I didn't want to open it. There was a newspaper, but I didn't want to hear that we were losing the war.

What I wanted least was the door of my office to open and my brother to walk in, but that's what happened next. Phil was a little bigger than me, a little older, a lot grayer, and a lot meaner. He was a Los Angeles police lieutenant who had seen even more than I had and didn't have the pleasure of sitting back when the case was over. Another ten cases were always on his desk. It kept him angry, but he had been angry even before he was a cop.

"You could have called me and Ruth," he said.

"I didn't want you to worry."

"She worried anyway," he said, loosening his tie. He was forever loosening his tie. "I could . . ."

And he could too. He could come in worrying about my health and get mad enough to beat the hell out of me.

But he looked away after taking one good stare at my cuts and bumps. Then he sat down in the single wooden chair on the other side of my desk. Something was on his mind.

"Nice day," I said.

He looked back at the photograph of us and our dad and dog.

"A little cold for this time of year," I went on.

"Shut up," he rasped. "I'll get to it."

I shut up and started to open my mail. It was all junk, including one letter that told me I could help beat the Japs by buying a series of one hundred cards showing the silhouettes of all Axis planes and warships.

"I want your help," Phil said softly. He bit his lower lip.

"Sorry?" I said innocently.

"I need your damn help," he repeated in a shout.

I looked at him and saw a face full of fury. He didn't want to do this, but it was something that had to be done. He might hate-love me, but he trusted me, trusted me more than his partner or maybe even his wife and three kids.

"You want me to help you? With what?"

It was coming hard, but he was determined it would come. "A friend is in trouble, needs help, a friend I used to know before I met Ruth." He had spit part of it out, and it tasted bitter. I knew he would hate me more when he was done, but trust was more important to him now, and he trusted me.

"She came to me for help, knew I was a cop," he said. "I can't help her. She has no case, no evidence. She needs . . . hell . . ."

"A private investigator," I supplied without a smile.

Phil turned his back and sighed deeply. "Right," he said.

"And do I know this person who needs help?" I prompted.

He said nothing, and I repeated my question.

"Mae West," he said. "It's Mae West."